CW00550780

Jen Calleja is a writer and literary translator originally from Shoreham-By-Sea, West Sussex, and now based in London. Her debut collection of poetry, *Serious Justice*, was published by Test Centre (2016), followed by the pamphlet *Hamburger in the Archive* (If a Leaf Falls Press, 2019). Her short fiction and poetry have appeared in many publications and anthologies including *Ambit*, *3:AM*, *Somesuch Stories*, *Funhouse*, *Another Gaze*, *Hotel*, *Structo*, *PROTOTYPE* and *Spells: 21st Century Occult Poetry* (Ignota, 2018), among others. She was shortlisted for the Man Booker International Prize 2019 for her translation of Marion Poschmann's *The Pine Islands* (Serpent's Tail) and was the inaugural Translator in Residence at the British Library. She plays or has played in the bands Sauna Youth, Feature, Monotony, and others.

I'm Afraid That's
All We've Got Time For
by Jen Calleja

for Richard

I'm Afraid That's All We've Got Time For

I need it to be perfect / I need it to be real
That's just what I'm saying / That's just how I feel
    from 'Perfect' by Murderer

Town Called Distraction

I loosely calculated faint figures in my hand.
The bridge to the east side of town would be
down and crossable for a quarter of an hour from
quarter past twelve, and for ten minutes at
twelve forty-five. Even if I were to make the
close of the first window, I would still be fifteen
minutes late, yet the second window glowed in
pink neon next to the faded twelve-fifteen. I knew
I would be distracted by the world. The world
requests time. I'd been listening to the news on
the radio before leaving and had to spring back
upstairs to note down names mentioned in the
broadcast to look up later on. The bus pulled in
while I was scanning the headlines in the newsagent's in front of the bus stop and I rushed out to
meet it. It had been the wrong bus, so I waited
and wondered how long ago the council had had
the bus shelter replaced, if ever.

Once on the correct bus I sat beside a woman
completely unlike myself reading a newspaper.
I sought out the important parts out of the corner
of my eye. I completely agreed with the style
of dress chosen by a French politician. I read all
the stories about America. I had to unpick the
tears sitting on my lower lashes after reading
about a memorial service up north. I didn't notice
the woman leave, but remember picking up
the newspaper from her empty seat to continue
reading it. My fingertips felt roughened and dry

from the paper; I looked around in my bag for hand cream. There is so much space between molecules that we never really touch anyone or anything. I moisturised more air than skin. As the bus took a detour due to the Carrutherson Pass being closed on Thursdays, which I'd forgotten about, I was notified that my book was ready to be picked up and would be available for the next three weeks. I got off a stop early to pick it up.

There was no one at the counter, so I went around the back to try and find someone who worked in the stockroom who could find the book. I'd ordered it because the blurb used a turn of phrase I'd always admired and I was half serious about highlighting any word in the book that I felt proved the existence of an ideology I'd been playing around with for almost two years. It started off as a miraculous discovery, a new way of seeing, but now it was the only way I saw, the only way I wanted to see. Not many others knew about it though, so I wasn't a fanatic, I was just very interested. The depot had a TV in the corridor outside the stockroom and I leant as if bored against its screen, with a flat palm on the end of my stiff arm, to twist my head and shoulders in for the thrill of guilt and culpability the inter-national news would give me. Television perfectly illustrates the theory of quantum physics; I birthed this *intellivision* in my head. Those pixels

everywhere in every colour being everything
– being there but not being there, I reasoned –
they could be everything, though they will never
be real, they will never really exist outside imagination. Possibilities mean so much more than
reality these days. They certainly do to me. If only
he wanted to confuse me or contradict himself
and smile because of it.

I started walking towards the bridge, but
very slowly. I was worrying, I remember, about
whether things would turn out alright in the end,
if things had already gone wrong sometime up
to this point. On the way I saw a cash machine,
but decided not to check my balance. It looked
a lot like an arcade game with its fully-flashing
colour screen, full quantum. Where is my money?
There's more money than there is money, there's
more money than is needed for the whole world
to be OK.

I thought of a joke I could tell if I thought he
was trying to make us feel serious. I read it
through in my head while my facial muscles held
a tech rehearsal. I knew I'd missed my chance to
cross the bridge, but by this I had saved myself.

Literary Quartet

I arrived at the entrance to the Literature House at the exact time set out on the invitation, turned my back on its facade, waded through the orange leaves on the opposing green, and climbed a tree. Sitting on a branch, I thought of the other short-listed writers already inside, the cameras roving around trying to capture their famous targets, the lights heating up, the countdown to showtime running ever faster.

I wish I could know what story I'm trying to write when I'm writing it, was the magnified quote underneath my photo in the concertina brochure for the prize-giving that they were handing out at the Literary Exchange. I scanned it over and over throughout the journey. I go to the Literary Exchange to write. It used to be Bridge Gallery, that building by the river as big and open and bright as an airport terminal. They left the final exhibition up when the place went bankrupt. Now the space is full of reclining armchairs, all pointed at different angles towards different garish, neon paintings. Each armchair is next to a small, cuboid bookshelf, where you can choose from a selection of volumes wrapped in uniform grey packing paper, covering the title page and colophon; inside, all traces of the authors' identities have been erased, too. I had read another Blank Book to focus my mind that afternoon.

After a surreal three years that began with my acceptances outweighing my rejections, and included winning a regional award, things were on the up – potentially stratospheric, depending on how tonight turned out. It was finally happening. Every year, for over twenty years, I had watched this historic occasion. The drama of it, the fuss, the prestige. I knew everything about the Prize of Prizes Prize; the compères, the scandals, the rumours, the *winners*. I still own a badge, jumper and notebook, all with the pre-1990s logo.

For the past ten years I'd wanted it in the opening line of my biography – and for it to be the reason I didn't need an introduction. Five years ago, I'd signed up for the offer to receive specially bound copies of each winner's book – always white, with black embossed font – as a way of affirming to myself that I, too, could be a winning writer.

Perched in the tree, under the street lamps' cold light, I stroked my fragrant, freshly conditioned hair. I had been to the hairdresser that morning. Someone wearing a headset waved me down from the tree and handed me a glass of sherry. I followed them inside the Literature House to take part in, and perhaps become, an institution.

My coat was whisked away, a microphone clipped to my dress, and I was ushered into the ceremonial hall. Swirling around its five zoned-off areas, one for each stage of the evening, were hundreds of gaudy, volatile people. Cameras zoomed around, intruding on conversations. I was led to the zone nearest the entrance. As I approached, the other shortlisted writers, standing around two corpulent beer barrels, fell silent. I air-kissed all three. The lights dimmed with an *ooooo* from the crowd and a spotlight descended on us as the compère of the last twelve years, Audrey Wollen, began the proceedings:

'Ladies and gentlemen, we're gathered here for the live, televised judging of the fifty-ninth Prize of Prizes Prize. Please give your warmest welcome to our four shortlisted authors: Bobi Entré, Thomas Grech, Hester Heller and F. F. Tine.

'Our three esteemed judges will soon commence their private deliberations while seated on the platform nearest the Victory Chamber, where the *exclusive* party for the triumphant author will take place after the winner has been announced.

'Each nominee's book will also be discussed live by the nominated writers themselves – peers among peers – in an attempt to persuade our eavesdropping audience that they are most deserving of the Prize.

'During the evening, each member of our four-hundred-strong audience – made up of readers chosen by ballot and special guest critics – will place a token in one of the centrally positioned glass vases, each representing a short-listed author. The tokens all have different values. Readers' bronze tokens are worth one vote. Critics' silver ones are worth ten votes. The writers' gold tokens are worth twenty-five votes. And no, they cannot vote for themselves – however much they long to. And, lastly, the author chosen by the judges will receive two hundred and fifty additional votes. Whoever receives the most votes overall will win the Prize of Prizes Prize, instant fame, glory, the works.

'But that's not it, for, as usual, there are also consolation prizes to be awarded. The unsuccessful author with the highest number of gold tokens will win the exquisite Writers' Choice Prize. The runner-up with the most silver tokens will get the coveted Critics' Choice trophy. And, for light entertainment, the writer with the most bronze tokens will take home the Public Choice gong. Should an author qualify for multiple titles, the judges will share out the goodies. And we promise that, unlike last year (and every other year), we will not throw a custard pie in the Public Choice winner's face.'

Tittering laughter, and one guffaw.

'So, with all that out of the way – let us begin… Evening Drinks with Canapés!'

Aperitif! Aperitif! cheered the crowd.

As drums rolled, two large silver dishes of oysters were placed on the barrels in front of us. Flutes of champagne were handed around as our four books, each on a silver stand, were placed by our feet. The crowd relaxed and began to edge closer, occasionally penetrating the spotlight. We slurped oysters determinedly and began our discussion.

'So, Mr Grech, Thomas if I may,' Bobi Entré smiled, tossing an oyster shell onto the sawdust-covered floor of the zone. 'A main character.' He let it stand.

'Yes,' Thomas Grech nodded, lifting his champagne glass.

'Don't you think having a main character has been done to death?'

I was proud to be here – and, I assumed, the others were too. We had worked hard and produced the finest works of the year, perhaps of our generation. We deserved this honour. But I, and maybe the others too, considered the nominations with some suspicion. I had to admit, I knew all three people who had got me on the longlist, which wasn't (technically) allowed. One was a publisher that I had read submissions for; another a non-fiction publisher who was courting me for a book; the third that well-meaning essayist everyone knows.

One of Hester Heller's nominators, an ageing poet, is the brother of her publisher's editorial director. One of the others is in her writing collective and shares her love of white space and absurd juxtaposition. A third taught her Persuasive Writing at university.

Bobi Entré's manifold sponsors included a Scottish novelist who he once had an affair with and a widely despised aristocratic author who writes working-class characters with cringeworthy dialogue.

As for Thomas Grech, he was already lambasted in the media for being a 'personality' before even a single word of his book had been published. Barely twenty-one. Part-time model. Did not give a shit about being championed solely by his father's friends, including one seventy-year-old writer who explained his choice: 'It would be great to have a meeting of minds – and to get a photo with him.'

Still, the nomination that I was most suspicious of was the public's, whose votes had whittled the longlist down to a final four after repeated televised adverts featuring jolly readings of book extracts with designated phone number extensions running along the bottom of the screen. What was their agenda? What did they gain? Did they just like the look of me? Had they read the review that said I was influenced by *that* monstrosity of a book? Did they know who my ex-boyfriend was? Or were they really struck by the two pages I had read while balanced on the roof of a river boat?

'And what about your process?' Hester queried.

'My process is embedded within an aesthetic of relatability,' Thomas enthused. 'I chose popular names from the past year, overpopulated cities, popular items of clothing, most-searched-for turns of phrase and words of the year, made sure to mention the characters are reading the latest bestseller and watching the highest-grossing films. My publisher also sent me their three-year plan of what their predictive focuses were going to be thematically, so I took from that as well.'

'And your next book?' Bobi asked.

'Oh, the same I think. But I'll…'

'…update everything…?'

'…update everything and then we'll do seasonal reissues.'

'Some of us were a bit confused about the length…' I ventured.

'Well, it's clearly just the first chapter.'

'Right, with some bullet points across blank pages to set out what people can expect?'

'Yeah, the book hasn't been written yet, but people are really excited about it. That's why we also submitted the Petition of Interest signed by everyone who *will* read it, once it's written.

Naturally, it's going to go through a few changes, like plot and… Oh, here comes father!'

Applause rose as the illustrious playwright Edgar Rosalvo Grech entered, followed by an assistant bearing a candle.

'Good evening everyone! I'm here to give the seal of approval to my son's book.'

He rocked a stick of green wax in the candle's flame, pressed the melted end onto Thomas's (mostly blank) book and stamped his dolphin-adorned metal seal over it, before marching off through the fawning crowd.

The retreating candlelight swam in the glass of the vases. They were darkly coloured, but I could make out that they already had a few tokens glinting inside them. Some people must have already cast their vote when they came in. The mounds of salt cradling the oysters glittered magically, sending a refraction of light onto the hand of my barrel partner, Hester Heller. It made her seem special, this gesture from the mineral. I could almost hear the sound of the sea, or applause off in the distance.

'And now, would the authors please… Join Us for Dinner.'

Be our guest! Be our guest!

The spotlight followed us to a large, round table with a white tablecloth while the band swayed against their violins. Red wine

22

was poured into mauve glasses. The four books were brought over and arranged as a centrepiece. Four bloody steaks were placed in front of us. I had told them I didn't eat red meat; was this a test?

'Hester, what made you tackle this particular subject?' Grech asked, a cube of meat readied on his fork.

'Hm, as you know, the collective I'm part of – Fresh Pillow – establishes leitmotifs and methods and styles of performative reading at our annual meeting and we all work from those as a blueprint. Our showcase portfolio will be coming out soon with profiles, photos, suggested "big work" and contact information for all twelve of us, and we'll open up our events diaries for appearances shortly after that.'

'And what other writers are you interested in right now?'

'Definitely John Free, Wendy Quaid and Tish Gupta. All exquisite and important writers.'

'And also part of Fresh Pillow?'

'Yes, yes they are.'

I had forgotten to have lunch. When my concentration lapsed again, my eyes drifted to the judges' zone.

Had I really been trying to ignore the fact that among the three judges was Charles?

The writer Charles Vivard had been a junior

23

lecturer when I was in my first year at writing school. After I finished school his reputation grew, and we had remained in the same networks – how could we not have.

A few months ago he had contacted me to say that he had pushed one of my real nominators, his publisher, to select me. The email had read: 'Don't worry about getting on the list, it's sorted… your greatest work to date… very proud.'

The morning's haircut slid into my mind, pressure set in around my shoulders. I blinked, forcing my focus back to the table.

'And what kind of writer do you want to be remembered as down the line, Hester?' Thomas was saying.

'I'd like to be a Rediscovered Author, so in the next couple of years I'm probably going to stop publishing my writing, store my unpublished work in an archive and then in a couple of decades my publisher will offer it up to a literary journal as an exclusive.'

Hester had been tipped for the Prize in certain circles five years ago, while still in her second year at university. That had been a difficult thought to handle the last couple of weeks. She must have had a dozen nominations, maybe more. I heard a rumour that her name had been engraved in the Victory Chamber while she was still a teenager and they had just plugged up the letter

24

grooves with white plasticine. A toothpick await-
ed the announcement: either this year, or next
year, or whatever year. It would come eventually,
and she was impatient for it while she was still
young. I had noticed toothpicks on the bar when I
came in. She had been shortlisted multiple times,
her nominations rising steadily each year, spurred
on somehow by the inevitability of it all. Everyone likes to back a winner. I needed to pick my
teeth, they felt itchy.

The ones who persevered, and didn't crack,
would get there eventually – unless no one liked
you, and I doubted anyone particularly liked me.
But this award breeds awards. More would follow
shortly after, including a couple of new ones
looking to establish themselves with the promise
of money... What was I even doing here? It was
impossible.

My head throbbed. The audience shifted as
my vision blurred. Everything around me seemed
to hint that it could be peeled back. Pulling up
the chair upholstery would reveal hidden papers,
I was sure of it; under the glass coaster and paper
doilies were notes written backward in pencil,
the floor tiles could be lifted, twisted, rearranged
to form a message. Looking down at the floor I
could already make out something, letters formed
by the grouting. It appeared that there was something written on the ceiling, in dangling cobwebs.

I focused again. Some of the audience were listening intently, others were gesticulating at the books, arguing, and one or two seemed to be sleeping.

Charles caught my eye from the judging corner. I smiled robotically as my hand nervously tousled my hair. While I had his eye, I mouthed: 'Which was your favourite part?' He replied with a shrug and a smile: 'I couldn't possibly choose.' Had he even read it?

'And now, Just Dessert!'

Sweet stuff! Sweet stuff!

I stopped thinking about it all while we moved zones to the tinkle of the piano. We all sank into plush, purple armchairs. A trolley bearing miniature cinnamon swirls dipped in powdered sugar and presented on translucent plates appeared. A ginormous piping bag filled with thick hot chocolate was lying over the shoulder of a chef like a fat baby. He encouraged florets of it into boiling-hot frosted-glass tumblers braced within wooden holders. The cold mixture gradually relaxed into a warmed drinking chocolate. The conversation had moved on, and I hadn't spoken for at least thirty minutes. I still wasn't used to the sweeping cameras and the hot lamps, to the crowd's relentless whispering.

We're in a labyrinth of ladders, arcing and curling around one another, following others' routes, occasionally being given a hand over

26

treacherous rungs. Some ladders end in dead ends, others lead to platforms from where we can shout down encouragement or ignore all those beneath us. No one knows how anyone gets up there, the routes are not well lit.

'Bobi, Bobi, Bobi, there was so much I loved about this book,' Heller said, blowing on her hot chocolate. 'There's the repeated use of the word "lush" that I really enjoyed. There was also the enchanting cadence of each sentence. And when Rizzo turns to Gregoire and says "You're as mad as a hatter!" that was such a great moment. But –'

Bobi licked his fingers.

'It's just a shame that this wasn't the book everyone was promised.'

'In what sense?' Bobi asked, thrusting his plate at a waiter.

'Well, in the sense that this is a translation by someone else, so it's not wholly your book. It would have been much nicer to have been able to read the original book.'

'You can read French?'

'No, no, I mean, very few people can, but it just would have been great to have read the *real* book. Or if *you* had translated it then we would have been…'

A very tall, thin man appeared at Hester's elbow: 'Lush! *Lush!* That was my choice! He wanted to use *moist*!'

27

'It's OK, Jerry,' Bobi said gently. 'She didn't mean it. Go have a drink and I'll see you later.'

The man looked on the verge of tears, popped the collar of his jacket and stormed off.

'And finally, Coffee Time for a little sober reflection and a final boost before the winner, and runners-up, are announced!'

Make it strong! Make it strong!

We 'retired' to the 'Drawing Room'. We squeezed onto the one sofa, balancing espressos on our laps, serenaded with the help of an acoustic guitar and a distant opera singer. We could no longer face one another, just the cameras in front, while the audience crowded around us. Someone said, 'Absolute farce'. Someone rested their hand on my shoulder and whispered, 'Writers are quite sensual, aren't they? Always having perverse thoughts. Want to go somewhere after this is finished?'

'To be honest,' Bobi began, as I shooed away the interloper, 'I wasn't convinced.'

He inspected my book, brought over on its display stand along with the others, for the final time.

'I like that the spine is slightly creased, but maybe it would have improved things if you'd just left it to gather a bit of dust or a bleach fade or something.'

My editor, Rossy, entered the spotlight and sat

on the arm of the sofa without acknowledging me. Bobi continued: 'Having read the original manuscript, I can see that you had to do quite a bit in an attempt to turn it into a book,' he said, tilting his head at Rossy. 'I really admire the work you've put in.'

Rossy smiled and nodded, raising her hand at the applause from the audience. She motioned to someone behind the cameras and the book cover designer, Saul, followed by the marketing team, came into shot, sat down crossed-legged in front of us, and began passing around a portfolio of alternative book covers. I felt hot and crabby, but at least I didn't have to speak.

Do I even like my book? If I really thought about it, large chunks of it were transposed from Blank Books I had been reading at the time of writing. I used the sentence structure and whatever level of disclosure was within them as a template and harnessed them to just write the loose story that I had. But you wouldn't be able to recognise passages or tell which books they were from. I used philosophy for ruminative moments. Gooey romances for sincere but accessible love scenarios. Gothic novels for landscapes. And the standfirsts of newspaper articles for strong chapter openings.

I know that it's all a sham. I don't even want it. If I won it wouldn't mean anything to me. But I suppose you can't stop it meaning something to everyone else.

Charles gave me a thumbs up. Charles blew me a kiss.

Charles had invited me to a gathering at his flat once. There were only three of us there – a guy I was openly seeing on the course, a close friend he was sparring with, and me. I said it was time I went home. Charles saw me to the door, and as I moved to allow him to open it, he lunged forward and bit me on my throat.

After that, Charles and I pretended that it never happened. It wasn't the only contact during those years. It was just the first. Now, years later, and it had all been forgotten in a way. Then he started offering me favours. And I had really forgotten it all. In a way.

That hairdresser, running the back of his hand down my neck, whispering 'beautiful'. 'He was overly familiar,' I had whispered to the manager as she helped me with my coat. I turned down the offer of a free haircut when she rang me an hour later to tell me she'd let him go. What would I be worth if I had accepted?

Charles sending me the email about the longlist had made me painfully rigid in my chair. Just the existence of this message felt like a trap I'd let myself fall into. I would owe him. His investment would need to be repaid, with interest.

I could have written back and said, 'I don't want it.' I could have confronted him, it was the first thing that came to mind, but then I thought: I deserve it. *I'm owed.* It's all a fix anyway. The prize is only a beginning. The hard work comes after. So I did nothing and then forgot it all, all over again. But there was no forgetting it now.

Strangers shouldn't be like that around you; that hairdresser, the hairdresser behaved inappropriately, he didn't even know me. I know Charles. I don't know, maybe we were just on different levels or something, in different worlds within a world, maybe it was a misunderstanding, but I know he genuinely likes my work, I know he wants the best for me and my work and he just wanted to give me a hand. But his hand, the hairdresser's hand, the touch of their hands gave me the same queasiness, made me absent, like the dog a child pinches when no one's looking, like new soft-furnishings; too good not to stroke.

'That's it ladies and gentlemen and our viewers at home. After a short break we'll be back to announce the winner!'

The vases were wrestled away to the stabbing strains of a cello. The tokens were to be counted before the judges made their closing remarks. The Prizes were being polished at the rear of the hall. The first announcement would be for the derisory

Public Choice Award. I was shaking all over.
There could be no victory. The other nominees
were climbing the steps to the stage. The VIPS
were slinking away to the Victory Chamber, they
didn't need to hear who had won. I froze. Then
I started backing away. I reached the exit.

I didn't hear the name they boomed that expelled me out into the street, back on the coach,
back home.

* * *

Watching the prize-giving online, I saw that when
I wasn't there to accept the Public Choice Award,
a shy but determined young man got up on stage
while the laughter was dying down, creaking the
softened spine of his copy of my book, massaging
it like a shallow accordion.

'I just wanted to read you my favourite bit, if
you don't mind…'

A dream I'd never dreamt before.

* * *

On Monday morning I went back to the Literary
Exchange. I was the first to arrive. The opening
manager looked at me in surprise through the
glass door. I looked away.

'Good morning, madam,' she said brightly with
a pitying expression. 'Can I bring you anything
to drink?'

I sat in my favourite recliner; a pot of mint tea arrived and was perched on a paper doily bearing a quote from the Prize's victor. I had stripped a copy of my book of its markers and wrapped it in the same grey paper as the other Blank Books. I slid it into the little shelf, stared for a moment at a neon pink painting with my eyes out of focus, and then closed them.

The Turn

The first.

The first bad thing happened before the morning was even over. I fell off my chair leaning too far to my right to pick up a ledger from the floor of the trailer at the harbour. I'll tell you, I was in shock. I landed on the bone of my backside – suddenly *there*, not *there*, looking up from the floor half holding the paperwork and everyone laughing at me.

I was lured onto the ships in spite of seeing injuries, corpses, zombified men, and hearing about the breakdowns, the broken homes, the mind games, the hallucinations. It had happened all of a sudden and when I had needed it the most. We all did. The wood mill had closed and moved, and we needed jobs within the month otherwise we'd all fall through a big hole. Mitchell had said the port, the harbour, but I didn't want to move cranes all day. Like I had a choice.

We walked down there together every day for five days hoping someone in the yard would be sick, really sick, for a couple of days at least so we could learn the ropes – or, even better, fired. On the Friday, the *Miranda July* was bounding in towards the harbour like a sheepdog in January snow and it was like witnessing an office coming to *us*, like a huge holy vision with the sun streaming behind it. We watched it come in and the crew get down, a couple of them bawling their eyes out, kicking at anything around them.

The uncle of one of the younger guys had passed away on the trip. His heart had blown and they were at least eight hours from land. They carried him down on a couple of planks wrapped in a few old sheets. No time to grieve, they had to set off immediately to go pick up some closer pots a few hours east before the whole trip was a waste. They hadn't been able to continue with him on board, he was weighing down the ship. I asked if we could help; two young amateurs could be a match for an old sailor. Like they had a choice. We were gone all day and when I got home to my parents' trailer that night around midnight I was a real person.

Once I had started, I kept going back for my hot crab bath. It brought something out of me; answers to questions I didn't even know I was asking came out of nowhere. A house with three bedrooms, a weekend trip away somewhere.

The clarity of our objective is exquisite. It makes getting up in the morning worthwhile; you could go home feeling satisfied and knowing why that is or go home dissatisfied and know why that is.

Communicating with Darlene was easy at first because she used to be out there too, it's how we hooked up. *Sounds like a really dangerous one, boy that sounds like a tough one.* But then

I realised that it wasn't professional. It would make the next four months leading up to the next thirty-hour shift unbearable, like Creggy, who had a breakdown. His wife too, eventually. He would run over all the possible scenarios. Drinking, pilling, his heart doing a dance. At home I liked scrubbing the table and peeling potatoes, sitting in my chair by the heater and reading the last two days' newspapers. In silence.

It really was like going to a different country, but where the place was like deep space, where time had stopped. I imagined that everyone else stayed asleep – I would leave and arrive home while they slept – and that a day hadn't been missed. My wife and children had been at home waiting. Not going on without me. *I use that day to pretend that you're dead*, my wife joked, leaning on her hand, her elbow on the armrest of the couch. *I imagine, well, I assume that you won't be coming back. I take the phone off the hook, there's no way to hear them calling to tell me, I already know, I won't be out of the loop.* I wondered if the children did that too, whether I died every time, whether they had stayed awake mourning me a dozen times. Did it stay in their little bodies, did it harden their muscles? And my wife, she sometimes looked at me differently, didn't she, like I was an imposter. Perhaps she had already mourned me the first time, all those years back. Maybe the worrying has affected all of the babies. She'd been carrying all the times I'd been out. Like the last time. Her stomach was large and hard-looking like a prize pumpkin.

* * *

I got onto the ships because of my uncles, cousins and brothers, of course. I had imagined the bedroom I shared with my sister was the sleeping quarters on a ship since I was a tiny girl. I could practically *feel* the swaying. They always tried to convince me that I was precious but I'd known that I wanted it since I was eleven. I ended up going to college, almost gave in to that tempting softness, but came back one summer, cut the bottom ten inches of my hair off and told them I wanted in. I didn't want to do it to prove anything, I just needed to do it.

They wrote 'GREEN' on the back and front of my jacket and down my waterproof waders. I bit the head off a mackerel and spat it out on the deck. *Way-o!*

I learned in college that crabs are part of our cultural consciousness, they're part of the contemporary imagination. People's ingestion of them is a private and social triumph. The consumption of them in huge quantities came after the B-movies, when the spaceships had landed in the cinema, the spider horrors, the alien fiends, the Little Mermaid's flirtations with Sebastian. *Batteries Not Included.* The consumption of fear, the eating of the unknown, that very special kind of egg you can crack open like when birds break open crustaceans, so much better than an oyster. Medusa's one million victims, Fisherman's wands, Jesus crowns. It's mythical.

The first trip with him, with Rudy, it was like the love came out of nowhere. In the first hour they all seemed the same to me. Stretched, pinched faces, all chain-smoking, all in their matching gear, flexing their damaged hands. But by the end I was staring at the back of his head. Every time he touched me, an accident? It made my head fizz. Literally life-threatening, that shift. He moved in with me a month later.

Another one!

Yes, yes, I say through a mouthful of teeth.

Number six?

No, seven actually.

We weren't going to go over four, but there you go. And I stroked Maja's hair to encourage her to sit back down in the stroller. Petra was asleep next to her, vulnerable in Maxi's old t-shirt draped loosely over her compact body. Maxi was moored with one tense arm to the handle of the stroller. Pablo was humming in a carrier on my back, like a bee buzzing around my head. Adrienne and Alf were at mother's. And number seven had its back to the world behind the curtain of my body.

It was a nice moment just then, bumping into someone. Nice but hard work. I never know what to say or do anymore. They would look at the babies and then me, the baby-me, my baby-self, my babied-self, and we'd talk about their one big life. Our one big life. My lists of interests are long, ancient, outdated. I have a recurring memory of sitting in a bar with friends with my hair straightened.

At first, I was relieved by his commitment. The hand on my knee in the bar soon became a seatbelt. Soon I was on lockdown, a hand on my shoulder when we were walking, an arm around my waist when we were talking with anyone else. He was always giving my conscience a test.

The first time was hard, I was tired from day one. When Maxi came, Rudy would never get up in the night. In the day he said it was best I stay in bed. It was like the bed was sucking all the life out of me. Unaware of time or space, whether I'd eaten or drunk, I didn't have to lift a finger or lift my head off the pillow. Everything was brought to me. Intimacy included. I would lie in exhausted silence and the stone-throwing of baby cries.

Four months later I was with child again. The whole nine months in bed. It's probably why Maja's so feisty – she was desperate to move.

I ended up giving birth in the same ward as with Maxi. I looked in the same mirror in the accessible bathroom while walking off my contractions and saw how pale and bloated I was, how my hair was overgrown and ratty. I felt a new compulsion and gave birth to Maja energetically, talking more than I had in months. I woke up from a year of sleep, and seeing Maja and Maxi together made me feel like the head of a team, the host of a party, a captain. Rudy didn't want to hold Maja.

Once Maja said, *Daddy's hand is snappy like an alligator*. Petra will only look at me when we come in to say goodnight. In fact, I don't think Rudy much likes the kids.

When he goes away, I feel lighter. I get out of bed. I eat at the table. I drive into town. I pick up the kids and swing them around.

He got back a few hours early once and I was in the backyard hanging laundry. I was only about four months pregnant with Petra.

What are you doing out here, get in the house, get back in bed.

He checks on me every fifteen minutes.

He wipes my mouth from across the dinner table and then helps me out of my chair. I managed it on the second try. The numbness makes me so heavy.

I am buoyant, but anchored.

* * *

The second.

When Darlene and I took that first trip together, when I first looked at her actually, the first feeling was a despising kind of anger. She was like an alarm signalling danger, for all of us. You know you can't have a woman on board. I started watching her. Then started really watching. I pulled her up when she fell instead of whooping. I gave her the last of the raw liver and the potatoes in the twentieth hour. I took a shorter nap so she could have a longer one in the bunk. I wanted her and I said she could keep sailing, but I changed my mind.

She takes care of the kids and picks them up after school if I'm not around or if I'm sleeping and she thinks that she's better than me.

I taste the crabs. I lick them to get that kick of seasoning at the back of the throat and in the nasal cavity and the sweet kick of remembering the taste of its meat on my tongue. The taste of a crab is the taste of the sea, the taste of a crab is the taste of family, death and a warning from the sea. A lick of shell makes you taste the sea waving, swinging a bell.

Our job is unnatural, stealing sea monsters, pretending we are invincible, maybe already dead and unrekillable, to fish for crabs. Crabs as big as a dog, the twins of camel spiders, God's hands we call them sometimes. Crabs we would catch in cages the size of old fisherman's cottages that have now shattered off the clifftops. We were prospectors for that 'orange gold', panners with our gigantic dishes in a raging river, skimming the surface of the ocean.

You could imagine the roar at the bottom of the sea, millions of these creatures pouring out of an underwater volcano, a procession of them chanting bubbles. Their scream in the boiled ocean was what made the storms. When they didn't want to die, they bubbled and boiled and the force would rise up, speed up, erupt into the sky and set off the clouds. Water communicated with water, the molecules in our bodies would start to vibrate, release more water, we would add to the storm with our own fear.

On the last trip, Mitchell almost went over and I haven't been able to get rid of that feeling like a permanent, invisible bruise, a hole in my stomach. Once, when I looked out of the cabin window, I saw visions of the crabs consuming the crew. Things happen. Trip over the anchor. A rope would get caught around someone's leg or neck or arm, someone would slip over, bang their head on the low door frames, get socked by a cage, cut their face on a flying crab, frost bite, fatigue. It was only a matter of time, but thinking of Mitchell stung in a place that only hurt for my children, and Darlene.

I started inviting him over a lot, while he took a break from it all. Darlene and him had worked on the ships together too, before we met. It's good to make him know he's not forgotten and I see her looking at him. I took him and Darlene out for dinner. Her mother looked after the kids and they both went to the bathroom, first her and then him, and they walked back through the restaurant together. I asked her why her face was red and she said that carrying this baby was making her feel warmer than usual.

She ate like the food, our company, the atmosphere, were all meaningless. She acted as if we weren't there at all. I know he's been to the house while I've been out risking my life. She sits and frowns and says nothing. It has to go. Later, in bed, she sits up with her hand spread like a creature over its twelve- or sixteen-week-old existence. I know it's not his. She's mine. It's mine. It's tainted.

* * *

We lie in bed and he has to get up in a few hours and he says that we don't have any money and that having another baby right now isn't good after all.

* * *

I am equipped with the screen of three in the morning, the unbreakable promise of sunrise, the

44

blurring cobbles, the sky's oceanic mirror reflecting the whole-wheat houses. I had a vivid dream last night; it was as salty as a premonition. From the trailer I go down the hill towards the port, my body tensed and steady, bobbing up and down. Everything is not its true colour, bleeding out and dulled by a blind black. I'm wearing the concrete boots of sleep. I pop a mint into my mouth as I tread out my roll-up. I'm thinking about how the wire pots might catch in the cut at the centre of my middle finger and little finger I'd got from the lip of a handrail when I see Mitchell smoking, rocking his brown duffel bag and cradling his swaddled sandwich.

The *Miranda July* is only held together by water, at the perfect tension. Clear, prismatic stitches quivering at every bold twist, meeting at every seam. That, and crab dust. I see it cloud up like birthday card glitter in my second sight whenever one is flung with all its arms waving and lands and I see it mix with our expelled breath – a tar, mucus mist with a hint of blood – emulsifying to a tacky glaze that coats the ship. Jerry, Sven, Chief and Frankie would be coming later, in about an hour. We climb up the wet ladder with its blistering paint and give the place a once over for drips, leaks, strange noises, drafts, puddles, cold spots. I run a broom one-handedly over the pipe room – chalking up marks on the floor with the cigarette butts and soda tabs. Mitchell is shaking the padlocks joining the cages together. I hear the chain of jangles resonating off the block of cages and I sing *only thirty more hours with that asshole, only thirty more, only thirty more.* Even the handle of the broom is wet. I wipe my hand across my chest and squeakily down my waders.

Out from the land and the world heading north-east we become a ghost ship, we're on standby, suspended from reality. We're all dead men. We all kind of ignored the fact that Chief would be dead within the next six to twelve months – he'd come out of retirement and that meant certain annihilation. He'd even had a minor stroke coming back into port for the weigh-in the last time. When he quit nine months previously he'd lost his nerve, started seeing everyone's skulls under their stubble and eye bags and bloated bobbled noses and I haven't told anyone yet but I see it too.

Up in the cabin I get a message sent a few hours ago from Darlene. She got it done.

I looked out and a wave like a wall glided over the deck, knocking over Sven. He was up again, a little heavier with water no doubt. Over the speakers I shouted *Woah where did that come from, get up, up, way-o* and one beat later the black grins, the wan eyes, clawed hands and duck-bill hoods were all snatched in the fist of a blooming sneeze of seawater as tall as the ship itself. Their tiny bodies were sucked into the sea and I shouted, not over the loudspeaker, *way-o*.

All gone. *Way-o*.

I had to join them, but I couldn't let the ship continue; it could hit land or another ship or a harbour. I thought of the crabs, too. I didn't want them to die and rot for nothing; they would never become cuisine. When the boat sinks the crabs could get out, but if they didn't they would be trapped. I was their captain too. I kept heading north, faster now, further than ever, pancake ice like empty jellyfish stuck beneath the surface, a million moons floating on their backs. Soon we'd reach the serious stuff, the chunks of ice like fat blades. I had to move fast. The wheel to the most extreme left and cable tied in place. Within about a minute and a half the crabs and I would hit a bank of ice, possibly, hopefully, at an angle. I left the cabin in my t-shirt and tied a piece of rope outside on the rail and held on to it like I was rappelling down the side of a mountain in an avalanche, I couldn't slide overboard.

I took off my clothes, my legs felt constricted with cold.

I shuffled thickly towards the crab door.

I shot down, clattering, my fingertips running through crabs' legs clicking and cracking like tree roots, down a rabbit hole waterlogged and invaded, grabbing helplessly to these living balloons of meat, slipping through their fingers.

The crash didn't come. We haven't hit the ice.

We were wombed together, the crabs and I. They would nibble and tear me from myself, I would live on in them and all who ate them. Eat me up.

Falling off of my chair wasn't the real first bad thing. Reporting Frankie for taking his tools home to HQ before he got in that morning just so I would get a bonus was. He'll most likely be fired when we get back this time. I see that now. The second bad thing that happened was that she listened to me. I see that now.

The third.

Not a bad thing at all that my body will sing and the crabs will show me no interest. I see that now.

* * *

I had been packing bags for me and the kids when I got a text message from Mitchell. *Where's Rudy?* He had left for work hours ago, I told him. He hadn't shown up and they had a guy ready to take his place. *You better let him on then*, I said.

Three days later when I heard a knock on the door, Adrienne opened it at my request, shouted from upstairs, and someone asked for her mother.

48

Part of me thought, tell her, it'll save me having to tell the kids, but I went downstairs and received a man and a woman. As Rudy had been missing for a few days now, an investigation was underway to determine his whereabouts. They asked me questions, I answered them. A notebook and a letter had been found on his shared desk that I might want to see. I read the letter and the passages in the notebook indicated to me while the children watched them watching me.

You might need to prepare for the worst, the man informed me, as kindly as he could.

Why? I asked. *I'm already expecting the best.*

I placed a hand on my still modest belly. Everything will be fine. I'm the Widow Darlene now, and Miranda will be arriving in the fall.

The Debt Collector

I'd been remarried about two weeks when I decided I wanted to leave. I was in the park reading Leonora Carrington's short story collection *The Debutante and Other Stories* before work, and I'd got to a paragraph on page fifty-six that I'd had to re-read about ten times. It was like the lines kept shifting and twitching, fading in and out and being replaced with new lines that would overlay the old ones, or flicker over and between the ones on the page. The lines addressed me directly. *Emmanuella, you should leave your husband. You don't have to stay, Emma, you should free yourself. You've just been brought up to believe marriage is sacred, it's not what you really want, Ella.* I shifted my bra strap back under the greyed work polo I wore at the seafood place and looked at the lake so I would have something to focus on while I thought about how I was going to do it.

Robin thought I was going to work – I was wearing my polo and black trousers and trainers, so it was fair enough of him to assume so – and I didn't tell him any different. Instead, I picked up the water bottle he'd refilled for me, walked to the end of the road like I always did, and got on the first bus that arrived. I rode it until it reached the end of the line about fifty minutes later, got off and had a look around. There were a few nice-looking houses, big ones, freshly painted white with big driveways. I walked until I came to a parade of shops: a newsagent's, a betting shop, a Thai takeaway, an estate agent, another estate agent, a charity shop. I went in them one by one and asked if there were any rooms or bedsits going above their businesses. They all said no, but on my fifth attempt the woman in the newsagent's came around from behind the counter, maybe nodding or maybe her head was just bobbing on her neck, and she ushered me with her silky, worn down hand out the back of the shop through a store room, and out into a yard, unevenly paved and stinking.

We crossed the yard to a set of metal stairs and she led me up them to a brown, sticky door covered in dents like when you press your thumb-nail into soft fruit. Through the door was a large room with a low ceiling, one small window with a broken blind, and through a door that looked like it had been kicked in once, I could see the whitish skin of the shower curtain and a slice of the beige toilet seat hiding in the dark. There were dusty brown carpet tiles on the floor and three squares of dark blue linoleum to mark out the kitchen, which was a kettle, a toaster and a fridge.

She had been using it as a breakroom and office, but she would rent it to me if I wanted it. It smelled damp, there was only a sofa with milky crumbs mashed into it, a glass coffee table with a hairline crack and a small fake pine dining table with a TV placed at one end. She told me what she wanted for it. I thought about my savings. I could afford the room for about six months if I couldn't find work, then all my savings would be gone. Me and Robin had both agreed to try and save a certain amount of money and then we'd open a joint account together. I liked that having no oven or microwave would make choosing what to have for dinner easier, I could sometimes sleep on the floor or the sofa or even under the table, I could sit opposite the TV while I ate meals. I paid her a month in advance in cash. Luckily, I'd been taking out cash and stashing it away for the last few months, perhaps instinctively. She scrawled something illegible on a piece of glossy receipt roll, which is what she passed me the keys in, like two silvery eels in newspaper, or a shiny oyster in its crinkly shell.

After she showed me the main entrance to use around the corner of the shop – a black front door leading to three separate white ones embedded in plasterboard walls, the most scuffed one leading to a narrow carpeted set of stairs up to my second door – I phoned my work standing on the pavement outside and told them I wouldn't be coming back because I was moving away. I walked around the area for a bit, there wasn't much there. I had a boiling cloudy tea in a greasy spoon, then got the bus home. Robin made us a nice dinner, pork chops and mashed potato, peas and gravy and mustard. We had cheap and sweet Neapolitan ice cream for pudding. Afterwards I lay on the sofa with my head in his lap, and he stroked my hair while we watched TV. My head would shake whenever he laughed.

Thursdays to Sundays I usually had night shifts. For the next four days I took clothes and other things to my little room far away in the evenings after dinner, getting back to the house at one in the morning, not greasy or smelling of oil and sweat. I would sit on the sofa in my secret room and watch TV eating a packet of crisps, or reading a book, or having a nap, or plucking my eyebrows to use up the time and to test out my new life.

'Your shirt smells mouldy, the washing machine filter must be blocked again,' Robin said on Sunday morning, sniffing the polo I'd draped over his swivel chair in the office. 'Do you want me to give it a quick hand-wash so it's ready for tomorrow?'

On the Monday I left for my usual lunchtime shift, Robin gave me a long kiss on the cheek and teased me about my lopsided bun which I'd done in a rush, pinching it and making a honking sound. I went and sat in the park until I knew he would have left to start work at the swimming pool. I went back to the house and filled a rucksack and a holdall with some final stuff, and wrote Robin a little note:

> To Robin,
> I won't be coming back. Don't come looking for me. It's for the best.
> Lots of love,
> Emmy

I left the note and cash for the next month's rent and bills under the dumpy vase he'd made me in a pottery class a few months ago, and I emailed the good friends I'd made over the last few years to say that I was moving on and wouldn't be in touch again. I left the house and posted the keys through the letterbox. I threw my SIM card in a neighbour's bin as I turned the corner at the end of the road.

* * *

I went back to my old house about two months later. I walked at a regular pace down the road wearing nothing that had belonged to me while I lived with Robin. The curtains were closed and there was a white A4 poster stuck to the living room window. It was a picture of me taken at a friend's barbeque last year with the word 'MISSING' above it, and some other words I didn't have time to catch. I wasn't missing, I'd left him the note, I had been clear. Then I noticed that there were similar posters, some fresher than others, on the lampposts up and down the streets around the house. When I'd first noticed the posters in my periphery I had taken them for missing pet signs. I left immediately.

I got a job at a bakery a twenty-minute walk away from my little room not long after. I'd got bored of staying inside all the time reading and watching TV and it could be weirdly and oppressively hot in there sometimes. Most importantly, I needed to stop using up my savings. I got into the rhythm of the job after a few weeks and I liked the people that worked there, Liz and Mohammed and Greta and Odessa and Dave. One evening about six months later, a Saturday night, I didn't want to go back to my room. I got on the bus and went down my old road again, and I could hear that someone was having a party, there was music and loud chatting and laughing. It was coming from my old house. I walked by very slowly on the opposite side of the road and paused to pretend to retie my laceless shoes. I thought I could see the back of Robin's head, he had his arms in the air. We'd never had parties when we lived there. He must be doing well. He must be happier now. I got the bus back to my room.

A year later I went to see the house again. It was a bright sunny day and I felt enough time had passed that I could be a bit bolder. I must look quite different now after all this time, but I wore the cap and loose-fitting clothes I wore to the bakery just in case. I walked past the house and saw that the walls in the living room were salmon pink and there were pictures on the wall. Robin must have moved away, I thought. I started walking back down the street when someone came out of the house. It was Robin and a woman and a Labrador on a leash he was holding onto. They were laughing, and Robin lifted the woman into the air and kissed her while the dog jumped and barked. It felt like the beginning of a new relationship. Maybe I was witnessing the very moment he had found someone else. He had never said he'd wanted a dog when we were together. Or that he preferred brown hair. I got back on the bus and never went back to the old house again.

* * *

Four years went by and my little room didn't change that much. I referred to it as my Nest. A couple of friends from work and from the local book group I went to visited it and they seemed surprised or even shocked that I lived there, but I liked it. When summer was coming to my little part of the world I started thinking a lot about swimming. I hadn't been since when I could get a discount at the pool Robin worked at. I had always liked that pool. I went to the newish clothes shop on the parade for older ladies and bought a modest turquoise and midnight striped one-piece and went to the big leisure centre two stops away on the train.

I had just rinsed myself under the cold jet poolside and was walking past the shallow end when I realised that I was walking straight towards Robin carrying a small child. We both stopped and looked at each other. The child was looking at the pool and talking to itself, making faces for all the characters in its mind. Robin looked at me for about thirty seconds.

'Hello Robin.'

He smiled, then frowned, then laughed, then frowned.

'I, no, I was going to ask why but... The police, all our friends, the note. The waiting, the hoping. Just. I.'

I didn't say anything.

'Actually, seeing you I finally understand. Yes. You're looking at me the exact same way, just like you used to. You weren't wholly there, were you? I thought you were over him, way over him and all that. All those thoughts. I really believed it. I thought we were really happy. You were always going to talk yourself out of being happy. I can't. I know it's not your fault, sweetheart. I'm not going to do this. I've got to go. At least I know now. Look after yourself, Emmy.'

He bowed his head so he wouldn't have to look at me anymore, the child didn't wave goodbye.

I didn't watch him walk off. I walked to the deep end, climbed down the metal steps like the ones outside my little room and lay on the surface of the water. The sound of splashing and screaming echoing around me was overwhelming. I looked up at the glass roof and listened to the muffled announcements under the water. It sounded like *Emmanuella, what have you done? Emmanuella, didn't you wonder why?* I might have been crying, or the water might have been running into my eyes, but you wouldn't have been able to tell which.

Divination

When the rain wept and wailed and hammered its wet fists against the fences and flung itself down on the grass over and over again for two weeks, everyone in the valley was dismissive of it. After it had blown itself out and made way for the sunshine and a warm breeze that made the trees clap and the bushes shuffle in anticipation, the rain was chided and forgotten about. But its uneasiness had just withdrawn to the hills, where it had concentrated, pooled.

The water that *came out of nowhere* over the brim of the valley skipped up the cracked tile steps of the school like a trailing coat and skated down the ground floor corridor into the art class-room. It licked half-sculpted heads, reconfigured collages, fought against the repulsion of water-proof aprons and candle-wax stars in diluting midnight-ink skies.

Taken off guard, the small group of students and their tutor tried ejecting through the fire escape, but the security chain had rusted into its bed, pinning it open only a couple of inches. Enough water could leave through the back to keep the flood at chest height – the teacher's chest – so he and the four girls had to climb onto the storage shelf, stepping onto once precious mulched paintings and sketches, using the apron hooks twisted into the wooden shelf columns as a leg-up to the top shelf only a few feet from the ceiling. They pushed vague papier-mâché forms, wiry maquettes and carved animals into the dark grey rivery guest with an absorbing, inaudible plop.

The sound was a constant waterfall yawn, like they were in a cove somewhere in America, the sun streaming in through the windows while the constant water ran over the flat-rock desks and rock-pool sink, giving the classroom the kind of deep clean it hadn't had in over a decade.

The girls had to bring out the most expressive sides of themselves to compensate for not being able to shout, partly from the noise but also from fear. They all hung onto one another, having not touched in years – not so much as a misplaced fingertip when reaching for the modelling clay or the scissors. They gripped the sleeves and knees of their young trainee teacher, grateful to him, and he felt indebted to them for making him feel awash with respect, duty and purpose. He praised them all every few minutes, shaking their hands as if handing out medals: *Young ladies, I am so impressed with your bravery… Sylvie, Elodie, Sarah, Amandine, you are doing very well, everything will be fine, we just have a little wait. Shall we all sing a song to pass the time?*, he screamed, grinning.

The impatient water turned back out of the classroom to join the new wave running around the corner to the history lesson. The girls were grabbed and thrown from their desks, swathes of water pounced off their chests and then bounded out of the open windows like foxes.

The teacher bundled a few of the girls together and hugged them to him while standing on his desk; tens of girls bobbed up in the swell, held and lifted at the waist, their chins rising as gracefully as their record-breaking jumps, their mouths in sweet 'O' shapes, their navy blue sailor suits dyed a teenage black. The large maps spaced along the back wall of the room started guzzling, choked, then lay upon the water in their new translucence.

Thank goodness the older, generally taller students were on the ground floor. The higher the floor, the younger the pupils.

* * *

Half an hour before the flood, Ernestine had been on the second to top floor being taught by Monsieur Dubois.

She felt sluggish, her eyes and neck were drooping. She couldn't concentrate through the heat and the throbbing fog that was lingering from another evening of late-night TV and texting and imagining a variety of ways to make Monsieur Dubois look at her.

When he caught her eye and smiled in the hallway or in class, every muscle in her body did the equivalent of grabbing her arm and whispering, *Did you see that?* A positive comment on her work would be a week of euphoria, something negative or even lukewarm would mean a month of devastation, of shame and self-loathing. Most of the time she felt invisible, but he could see her.

Why do you have to look shocked, like the girls in magazines, to be beautiful? she thought. When she tried it in the mirror, she looked like someone had jumped out at her unexpectedly. Mouth slightly open and eyes wide: *Don't toddlers look like that after seeing a magic trick?*

She practiced this look subtly at her desk as a beacon for him, but it turned into a yawn. She had been experimenting with eyeliner lately and remembered while looking in the noir sheen of her phone down under her desk that Madame Camille had made her wash off her sophisticated flicks before class, leaving her with smudged, sleepless eyes.

She would watch anything on TV that seemed to have even the vaguest chance of having something erotic in it at some point. Old repressed vicars broken down by the sensuality of the teenage daughters of their clergy; girls pursuing married men for months, unable to think about anything else, even studying; visiting former schoolmates of parents who were foppish, cool and flirtatious; teachers ravaging their pupils after school. The girls were always so long-limbed, and could hold eye contact.

She spent a lot of time in her room watching TV, sometimes from after dinner until one or two in the morning, especially in the summertime when she couldn't sleep, without her pyjamas on, watching things she wasn't meant to watch. She had worked out how to switch off the timer her parents had set years ago. She had been staring into the TV for a long, long time – she was in dialogue with it. She had been restless since she was in primary school, fidgety, distracted, and the TV started presenting her with things that made this pleasant agitation peak. It started to even initiate it. *Is this what you like, Ernestine?* it seemed to ask her.

In the summer she felt like she belonged to everyone, and that she wanted to be near everyone. She felt drawn to every living thing.

Sometimes she felt like she wasn't made of the same blood and skin as the other students. She felt like she was in a spaceship looking out of the front window at the world and everyone knew she wasn't real. Mimi and Suzanne *did* make her feel real. They worried about her. *Ernie,* they would peep when they could see her drifting off into her own thoughts. *Ernie, let's all go to the beach this weekend. Ernie, we love you.*

'Ernie, we can wait for you?'

Mimi looked concerned and annoyed.

Monsieur Dubois had asked Ernestine to stay behind at the end of the class, enthusiastically, without looking at her and without saying why; he just began talking slightly erratically about the similarities between mathematics and literature, how they create spaces where anything could happen. She nodded, elated at his request rather than his statement, and he said that he was pleased that she agreed.

She packed away her notebook and pens, half reading the eight-ball prophecy that loomed up on her phone from Patrice at the boys' school a few miles away: *Photo? xx*

'Ernie,' Suzanne repeated, 'shall we wait outside for you?'

'No,' she drowsily waved off.

They both filed out, laying a curse on Monsieur Dubois as they left.

Monsieur Dubois kept looking at her arms and legs while he piled up textbooks, perhaps at the fine white hair sticking straight up and out and catching the sunlight. Maybe at the down on her face, like a baby has, that baby's lick off and eat. She looked down at her arms. Was the hair a continuation of her blood vessels? They hadn't been taught that, but why do we have hair on our bodies? She wiped a sweaty hand down her sweaty leg.

She liked being around Monsieur Dubois but also found him repulsive. In turn, she found the repulsiveness of him attractive and somehow correct. She noticed that his nose and forehead were greasy and she acknowledged to herself that she was not greasy.

'Would you come to my office with me, would you help me carry some books?'

'Yes, of course, Monsieur.'

* * *

His office was in a former science lab on the ground floor. He swung open the windows to suck out the stale air. He asked her to sit down with him at his desk and he started saying that she was a real talent and that he could help her improve even further.

He placed only two fingertips – not a palm, not a hand – on her upper arm, tapped them unperceptively. She couldn't hold his look, her head was fixed downwards as if her neck had locked up, embarrassed, exhilarated.

'You are a joy to be around, my top pupil. We need more like you, we need you to be an example, and we will have to work very hard together. You get my lessons, you always fulfil your tasks exactly as asked. I've told my wife about you, we've been talking about you. It's hard being a teacher, so much responsibility, sometimes people don't listen. I'm so pleased about you. There is something about you, do you know that? You must be able to see it! Of course you do! It's such a relief to be out of that classroom and here, with you.'

She felt constricted, she felt dangerous, powerful; was she *his* now? She felt the age that she felt she was. They were having an adult conversation.

'Please, call me Bernard. But not in the classroom. I'm worried about you though. I'm worried you might lose focus. We must start right away.'

He touched an opened envelope on his desk and tucked his frizzed-out hair behind his enormous elephant ear.

Adults always look tired, but he looked *really* tired. His clothes looked as old and as tired as he did. She imagined that underneath his clothes he was wearing all the clothes he'd worn on all the previous days she'd seen him. Did he sleep, did he eat?

She was amazed that she had created this reaction in him. She sat on her hands and looked at the desk, nodding out of sync with his boomed words and his conducting hands. She was so overwhelmed that she could hear a roar in her ears. *Is this what happens before you faint?* she thought.

She could smell the sweat emitting from the greenhouse of his opaque white shirt. The sound

seemed to be rumbling out of her own body.
Or was it from the dips in the floor set with drain
grates for washing the burnt-red tiles, a dozen
of them like eyes?

The odd dripping and gurgling coming from
down below gave the room a dungeon quality
of coolness. Words started coming out in a cres-
cendo of his desperate eagerness.

'So, I was thinking about how you live very
close by – across the park? Yes, well, I thought
that maybe this weekend, tomorrow, you could
simply walk across the park and we could –',
he coughed, twice, 'go over some quite complex
things that the others in the class just wouldn't
understand, your parents must be busy on the
weekends anyway and most probably wouldn't
even notice you not being in the house, a young
lady of your age must come and go as she pleases,
I think I've seen your late night comings and
goings –', he wagged his finger and giggled while
grimacing, 'and, and, and…'

The 'and' was reverberating, becoming quieter
with every repeat; she seemed to be tilting backwards at the same time. He swallowed and dryly
said her name while casually, mechanically,
reaching his hand out towards her, his hand not
attached to him.

He fixed her with a horrified stare; he could
hear the roar! He could read her mind because

she was staring at him so hard. But then he looked at the door. Water!

There was a thud against the door – he must have *shut* the door – but the water squeezed itself underneath, around and even over, pressing in to join them, spurting with enormous pressure in massive arcs into the room like clear rainbows.

It ignored the step down from the door and came gushing across the floor, swirling, dancing, shimmering, crawling around and under the workstations, pooling around Monsieur Dubois' desk, splashing him playfully, bathing their feet.

Ernestine windmilled her arms and fell backwards off her chair, the stream of shrieking water already a foot up off the floor; it hit her in the eyes, weighed down her arms. He was shouting her name, questioningly, as if she had caused this interruption. Then he was screaming it as the crowd of water rushed them, whisked her up and chucked her straight out of an open window, sending her sliding in a torrent of bush-prickled water down into the continuation of the valley behind the school.

Au revoir, Ernestine!

* * *

She was sucked downwards like a handkerchief sacrificed at the set-sail farewell – *pop* – far, far

70

away, rolling on the surface of the thundering water, trapped inside a mirror in flux.

Hours and hours went by, she stole a gasp of air whenever she felt the wind like warm breath on her face. She dreamt of her parents, walls, chairs, eating breakfast, blue sky, beach holidays, feeling bored, Monsieur Dubois. *Would he have escaped?* she wondered.

She ricocheted off of things natural and synthetic and sharp, parts of her body ached, she felt winded, there were bits of her that stung as if bleeding. She imagined these cracks in her skin smoking like dirty paintbrushes in jam jars of water.

Paper and leaves and tissue and plastic stuck to her, she slid across the roofs of cars, got snagged momentarily on a cluster of tangled bicycles. She was just debris, mixing with other debris. Preoccupied eyes fell upon her in the swirling mash without realising what she was. A bin-liner, a piece of rubbish. She was kissed all over by plump baguettes bobbing around her like ducks.

* * *

When she finally came to a stop her face felt frozen, taut. She had no energy left. She was in pain. She blinked shallowly; something was sticking her eyelashes together. She could only

71

see a few grey inches in front of her. She tried harder and could make out fields of water, she was hovering above them. *How long will it take to walk through the park tomorrow?* she wondered without feeling. *I better get home, my parents might already be home* – (Her mother was on a halted train four hours out of the city, anxious in the middle of the submerged countryside, trying to get through to their house phone but with insufficient signal. Her father was pacing around their house half-dazed with the flu, holding his car keys in one hand and his portable radio in the other, wishing he could drive to the school, knowing the roads would be closed and that he too could get stuck. He had woken up from a fever dream half comprehending that his daughter's school was being read out in a list of those affected by severe, sudden flash floods that had been on repeat for hours.) – but she was being held in the responsible arms of a tree and could not move for fear of it releasing her.

She felt *unalone*.

She turned her head very gently and saw a grotty cushion with a soft-toy face. What was once a sheep was lying in the tree above her. She felt like being friendly.

'Bonjour,' she mouthed at the sheep's head.

It didn't respond. At first. Its mouth was smashed up, like a rotten log chipping itself to pieces. It slowly seemed to be testing whether the bits that made up its mouth would hold together, and then, finally, it mumbled:

'Bon. Jour.'

A mite skated over the surface of its only eye.

'Are you OK?' Ernestine clucked out the question in her throat.

'I'll. Be. Fine.'

It took a few minutes to process these words.

'I don't feel well.'

She felt too tired to nurture a tear. Her exhale was a shallow, almost imperceptible draft.

'Stay. Still.'

They lay in silence for a while, an hour, two hours, not looking at each other. Then, her thoughts seemed to come out directly as speech.

'Do you think Monsieur Dubois is... alright? I shouldn't have left him.'

'You wanted to leave him.'

The sheep slurped on its words.

'I... didn't?'

A pig was hanging in the branches above them, heavy as a rubber thundercloud, its tongue hanging like a deflated balloon out of its mouth. She whispered:

'I wonder if it's listening.'

'You should have. By the way.'

The sheep coughed, dribbling black blood into its woolly goatee.

73

'*You should have wanted to leave.*'

'I like him.'

She muttered it almost inaudibly.

The pig's tongue disappeared up behind its teeth and it boomed:

STAY AWAY FROM HIM

Its chewy voice echoed over the plain of water. Saliva ran out of its mouth onto her shoeless foot.

'But… why? He… likes me too. He makes me feel… *good.*'

A trio of skinned rabbits, presumably from the butcher's or a nearby farmhouse, glistened in the tops of the tree like oily pigeons. They tweeted every now and again:

G i v e m a m a a k i s s !

G i v e p a p a a k i s s !

The sheep's eye did nothing.

'*Ernie. Listen.*'

STAY AWAY FROM HIM, the pig rumbled again.

'*He is not your… friend. He is trying… to trick you. He wants to be… alone with you.*'

'I want to be alone with him.'

G i v e g r a n d - p è r e a k i s s !

'*You want to… share a secret with him. That's…* OK. *You can't stop… thinking about him. Like that sports presenter that's… on* TV *all the time. What's his name. Bruno Petit. That's* OK *too. You want to… continue feeling. Fine. Just not with him.*'

G i v e y o u r s p e c i a l u n c l e a k i s s !

*'It won't stop where you… hope in your heart.
His praise won't… last much longer. You won't…
want him in all rooms in broad daylight sober and
in all weathers…'*

'Stop patronising me. I'm not a… child.'

*'There won't be a… bed and… candles and…
roses and… conversation, he won't be wearing
his…* shit *suit. It will be in his… living room
or a… kitchen or a… utility room.'*

'I want…'

*'It will be in the… morning or lunchtime or the
mid-afternoon. He'll be in his… weekend track-
suit. You won't feel* like *it. He will. It cannot be
undone.'*

HE'S AN ARSEHOLE

'He's not.'

DISAGREE

'He just doesn't want to… play by the rules, he
thinks they're not for him. He's like a king burning down his own castle.'

DON'T TRUST HIM

She looked down through the branches to the
water, and saw her podgy red face scribbled out
by her black hair.

*'When he looks at you, you feel like a…
woman. When he looks at you he sees a… little
girl. A pet. A challenge. A fix. You're not yet in
the age of lovers. You should be able to* laugh *at
a lover. Over*power *them. Feel safe even in the*

75

deliciously perilous *moments. You can* tease *them.*
Argue *with them. They shouldn't be able to hold*
you *being* you *against* you. *Or call you a* liar
in public and ruin your life at any moment. Please,
keep it all for yourself, for as long as you can.
You can trust *yourself. You will not let you down,*
or lie to yourself, or misunderstand things, or
change your mind on what the deal was, or hurt
you. Give yourself *everything that you're feeling.'*

HE SHOULD KNOW BETTER
'Ernie, do you know how heavy a man is?'
E n c h a n t é e !
'How do you picture it happening, from above?
From the side? Can you picture his real face right
now?'

I r e w a r d a l l m y l i t t l e w o r k e r s !
'Will you both spend supper with your family?
Has he seen your collection of bears? Your post-
ers?'

HE SEES THAT YOU THINK YOU'RE WEAK
T h e r e – t h e r e , t h e r e – t h e r e !
'You are curious. You won't resist. You don't
even know what *it is you would be resisting.*
You haven't experienced the aftermath *of count-*
less complicated situations. You've not yet
experienced your self breaking. *Afterwards you*
will justify it, even if you feel a certain sadness.'

'I… won't regret it if that's what you mean.
I have to live.'

76

'You will. It will all come to pass. But on better terms. Maybe with Patrice. Maybe someone else. Maybe no one. You think this *is living. I understand why. But it's like nuclear waste, it's like setting a cliff off crumbling, it's like turning over a sand timer. The memory will start off small and even maybe warm. Then your brain will adjust, but will have to do so around it...'*

I t h o u g h t w e w e r e f r i e n d s ? !

The sheep suddenly got more and more worked up.

'He should be like a third parent *to you! Better than a parent! A* protector, *a* confidante! *He should want you to grow, and help you to! There are laws. There is protocol. There are contracts. You don't have to worry about those.* He *does! His name is all over these things. Not to mention the unspoken rules. He shouldn't be so* selfish.'

I ' l l g e t y o u o u t o f t h i s m e s s ...

'But... But sometimes teachers and students fall in love and get married.'

Ernestine mumbled this without any commitment at a slowed down speed, like a worn-out video, her eyes closing.

'The world has offered you a lie. Maybe both of you. But I don't care about him. I care about you.'

... I f y o u d o m e a f a v o u r !

'He's pushing against a world he feels trapped in. It's all for him. And afterwards, you will be...'

77

Ants were working through her hair whispering the sweetest things. Something heavy and half-formed, like a pebble or a bubble, dislodged from the back of her mind and settled at the front of it. And then she fell asleep.

* * *

Ernestine woke up in the backseat of a farmer's truck, covered in a coat pungent with animal dung, moving at a crocodile's pace through water in the dark.

My poor Moutony, poor poor Moutony, the farmer's hat muttered to itself over the low radio.

A bundle of wool and legs could be made out in the trailer through the thin, rectangular back window, spattered with dry mud like flicks of plaster of Paris.

* * *

At the hospital, with her worried-sick mother and sick-shuddering father asleep in chairs by her bed, she was exhausted but wide awake.

She felt feverish. She found herself in the en suite staring at her miraculous pink body in the mirror. She was bruised, nicked and grazed. She felt strong and calm and like an old friend.

* * *

The school almost fell apart after its vigorous wash. A makeshift *learning environment* was set up in the form of a series of raised portacabins perched on the residual water in the games field. The students would avoid alligators by jumping from wooden pallet to wooden pallet from the driveway to the jumbled row of huts.

On her first day back at school six weeks later, Ernestine looked out for Monsieur Dubois. *He better be the one looking out for me*, she thought. *He better watch out*. She had had a long time to think and had a lot to say to him.

All the teachers were lined up on the driveway of the damp school in rubber boots and coats – all of them apart from one.

'Madame Camille, where is Monsieur Dubois?'

'Ah, hello Ernestine, I'm glad you're feeling better! I'm afraid Monsieur Dubois got very sick after the incident and he'll be taking a long rest. We're not sure when he'll be back. Hurry now, your lesson is starting soon!'

Ernestine wearily took on the pallets, hopping like a sulking frog across lily pads, slightly behind Mimi and Suzanne, and just in front of some older girls who were speaking very loudly and stepping on Ernestine's heels.

'Did you hear about what happened to the *sale type*?'

'Which one?'

'Dubois.'

'No, what?'

'My papa and the rest of the firefighters found him on the roof of the school the day after the flood. He'd climbed up the drainpipe. He was only wearing a vest and his underpants and was covered in cuts. But that wasn't the weirdest part. Get this: he was talking to some dead pigeons and a half-drowned cat and a mouldy rat. Saying all this stuff about how he knew it was wrong, that he was sorry, and all this fucking scary shit about a girl at a school in Lyon and he kept shouting: *Call the police! Call the police!* Apparently he's still in hospital, but my mama saw his wife and daughter driving off in their car with suitcases and boxes…'

'Good riddance to the creep. Did he say anything about Sophie?'

'Don't know. I wonder if she's had it yet?'

At the crossroad of pallets leading to different cabins, the older girls took a left with their arms tentatively around each other, as if trying it out. Ernestine stopped for a moment and watched them, then carried on heaving her heavy body to her classroom.

Suzanne held the door open for her, and Mimi leaned forward and offered her a hand up.

Befriended

Reinhardt Vogel, leaving behind his already elderly parents and an older woman he didn't want to settle for in Germany, flew the coop, became Richard Fogel, and arrived in Sheffield in the 1950s aged twenty. The triumphant anecdote that went with the duelling scar from his schooldays was willingly replaced with a fabricated tale of vaulting a chain-link fence and catching the corner of his mouth on a flailing piece of wire when he was fourteen and growing up in a well-to-do part of the Edinburgh outskirts. Sheffield was only meant to be a stop-off, but he fell into lecturing at the university (fell for twenty-two years) and then, quite late in his life, moved in with a girl who worked there as a cleaner. She had a son from her short-lived marriage to a policeman. He was pleased when he let her move in. He had been a little worried about the kind of house he would choose, and whether he would subconsciously pick a tall, grey *Wohnung*. He was also overjoyed to have an English son, and one that was so wonderful. He was over twenty years older than Audrey, and by the time Stephen was eleven, he was the same age that his father had been when he was Stephen's age: sixty-one. He had been Stephen's father for ten years and had baffled Stephen's biological father with words like 'consistency', 'stability' and 'stimulation', so the chap stayed away. They

would see this young and now portly man doing
his rounds on the high street and all would be
very polite and say hello and he would shake
Stephen's hand and return the nod that Professor
Fogel would direct at him. Audrey would ask,
'Y'alright?' in a neutral, closed-ended way and he
would echo it back. This was when televisions
made everything look dull, especially the people,
walking around doing dull things, never going
anywhere. When Stephen was approaching
twelve, he asked his father if they would visit
where he had grown up: the small farm where he
had run around and his mother had scolded him
about his mucky clothes.

* * *

Katherine 'Käthe' Griffiths finished school in the
summer of 1986 and moved away to the same
town in Bavaria that she had visited on a school
trip the year previously within weeks of getting
her exam results, telling her parents she had got
an admin job at an English company through the
parents of a school friend. In less than five years
she could get away with telling everyone out there
she was from Augsburg. She had barely said five
words in her first sixteen years in Llangollen,
but in Southern Germany the words flowed. She
drifted into driving a delivery van, lugging crates
of beer to bars all over Munich. After work, she

would drink in the bar next to the depot and be the loudest at telling jokes and would hold her loud laugh for minutes on end. Then, when there was a tricky situation with the wife of one of her fellow drivers (a very good friend of hers and a lovely guy) she asked for a job directly from the supplier to drive an LKW all over Europe. Her day spent in the cocoon of the truck's threadbare deep-red velvet cab was heaven: she was serenely at peace from the moment she woke up at 4 a.m. to drink her coffee in her small, yellow-bright kitchen in her fresh knickers and wet ponytail, to when she returned home a few days later. The front door opened onto the kitchen, where she would kick off one boot, put her arm out to turn the oven on, kick off the other boot and then shower while the oven preheated for a pizza. She would eat it while either watching repeats of *Wer wird Millionär?* or playing her games console. Driving was like sitting at a forever roving window. She never really noticed the road but saw the detail in everything around it. It was like going on holiday but bringing your bedroom with you. The concert stickers on the dash were peeling – in some cases only the sticky residue remained – and the patchwork quilt for roadside naps was perpetually crushed in the passenger footwell by outdated maps. She always had a cigarette on the go, ash sometimes dropping into the can of coke holed up between

85

her navy-jeaned thighs. She used her drinks
– sometimes sparkling water, no qualms about the
odd Helles if she was going to be in the middle
of nowhere for quite a few hours – to measure out
the time between stops. For the past twelve years
she had mainly been sent to France, Holland,
Italy, Spain, the Ukraine – rarely to the UK. After
coming back from Bulgaria, she had a voicemail
letting her know that in two weeks she would
be heading to 'Vales' for the first time since
she left.

* * *

He would have to see if they could find the time,
he told Stephen. Audrey would find it hard to get
the time off work; she still worked three days a
week, even though he told her that she didn't have
to. Stephen asked his mother if she could write a
letter to his school asking him to have time off for
a family holiday and she frowned automatically,
repeating that she didn't really like travelling, that
it would be quite a few hours by train and could
be quite expensive. Richard was looking into
what attractions this place had in some tourist
guides at their local library when a strange thing
happened. He started to feel panicked. He felt
wholly uncomfortable. He had perfected his
accent and language by watching war films and
through befriending an Englishman who worked

as the caretaker at the office where he briefly
worked when he was nineteen and planning on
leaving Chemnitz. The man was making a fresh
start after getting out of prison and had ended up
in Germany, specifically there. They met every
Friday evening for four or five hours and Richard
would use up his wages buying him drinks while
surreptitiously making notes under the table and
truthfully agreeing with him that Germans were
odd. When he arrived in Britain he was surrounded by information to absorb – gestures, stances,
hairstyles, typical topics of conversation – and
soon barely anyone commented that they couldn't
place his accent or that he was 'very European'.
He would lie about where he was born, where he
was from, where he studied. He knew that the
administrator who had processed his application
to join the university would be leaving soon,
and 'forgot' to present his identification when he
was offered the job. He kindly offered to step
in as an admin assistant in the interim. He wrote
his own story on the office's old typewriter and
slipped it into his file. He could tell his colleagues
of his unusual journeys around a slew of northern
universities for short periods of time, never
making friends. He had already visited the places
he mentioned and looked up older photos and
prospectuses for the periods he would have 'been'
there. He never worried about being caught out.

'We will visit the place where I grew up,' he told Stephen while standing at the dresser dusting Audrey's collection of china figurines while she rehung the curtains after a smack out in the yard.

* * *

A batch of mushrooms was clouding up before a seemingly randomly placed bench in the corner of the play park pointing away from the equipment. All curtains were open, every house immaculately tidy and no one to be seen inside or out. Her house in Munich was similarly situated: in a valley, pines piled up to the sky on all sides. Instead of an all-seeing wind turbine soundlessly turning in the wordless quiet, there were white Monopoly houses emitting puffs of After-Effects smoke. There were even more trees piled up on top of the pines, impossibly high, with impossibly placed mining cottages and leaning fields with sheep the size of grains of puffed rice floating like slow-moving cloud cars over the flat-coloured terrain. It didn't matter that she hadn't been back to Wales for twenty years; a day in the village felt the same as it always had: like a German Sunday, only the blinds were open.

'Oh, hello Katherine,' a woman standing on the pavement fingering flowers hanging over the low wall shouted cheerfully. She had glanced up on her approach, and then looked back at the drooping leaves of the plant. In a mauve overcoat over moss-green overalls was her Auntie Mai. She had been Käthe since moving to Germany, she was only called *Kat-trin* when visiting the serious atmosphere of an officious *Amt*.

'Coming in for tea then?' her auntie said, and she turned off down the path to her left.

* * *

He wrote some letters and made some phone calls from phone boxes. 'I'll book the tickets,' he told them when they asked if they would buy them on the day at the train station. They would take a week off from work and school. A week seemed like a long time off for Stephen. Professor Fogel wrote a letter to his teacher requesting time off for family reasons, and they allowed it. He bought the tickets – which didn't cost that much – at a travel agency in town. He kept the envelope in his office, in the top drawer of his desk, until the night before they were going away. The envelope felt hot when he took it out of the drawer to bring home.

* * *

She drank the tea – the milk overly present in her mouth, thick and sour-tasting – which she tried to mostly suck up with the crumbly biscuits on offer. She had the uncanny feeling of being in a suffocating dream.

'The magnolia's been doing awfully well in the wet weather, but the wall petunias are getting a little drowned. The post office might be closing and the Christian Centre has stopped selling cake so I won't bother making so many anymore. Baking's a bit of a fuss, especially since we had the kitchen made smaller during the renovations a couple of years ago. My wrists get bloody tired from whisking.'

Her auntie's voice was very quiet and slow, a gentle hum reverberating around the lounge like a radio playing in another room. Käthe couldn't remember when her stomach unclenched, or when she sat back against the cushions, leaning one pink arm on the armrest, like when she stuck her elbow out through the open window of the truck. She couldn't remember where the ham and mustard sandwich with a side of crisps on the small plate in her lap came from, or when the fire was reloaded with wood. She suddenly spoke – her voice deep and unrecognisable and suddenly in English – to say that she didn't think the traffic through the village was that big of a problem, and that she drove a truck for work that was currently reverse-parked into the dead-end by The Old Trout. It was suddenly dark outside, as revealed by the only small triangle of window left showing between the recently – when? – closed curtains. They ate stew with bread and cheese and watched a wildlife documentary. Her auntie chucked her an old patchwork quilt on her way up to bed, shortly before Katherine fell asleep in front of the television's static downpour. She dreamt she was trying to say something to her mother, who was kneeling in the garden aggressively pulling weeds from the beds. Her mother turned and placed a dirty gloved finger to Katherine's lips, just as her closest schoolmate's older sister opened the gate and said 'What are you looking at?'

* * *

It came to the morning of going away. The taxi would be arriving in the next few minutes. Audrey hadn't liked France, and he wondered what she would make of Chemnitz, especially when it wasn't in Scotland. The clock struck six. Richard knelt down before Stephen and zipped up his jacket. 'You can be whoever you want to be when you're older, but it doesn't mean you have to forget who you were as a child.' He told this to Stephen and kissed him on the forehead. There was a merry knock at the door: *tap tap-tap tap tap*. Stephen told him that he loved him. 'Your child-hood is where you start, and it is where you return,' he said, straightening up and opening the door. He would show Audrey their mismatched passports in the cab and point out how he thought the colours complemented one another.

The Natural

When he heard that the great Maltese actress
Marianne R. was coming to Glasgow to give a
series of masterclasses, Willem applied immediately. He was invited to audition a few weeks
later by letter and had to plead with his agency
to move his cleaning shift at the university. After
all the fuss and rehearsing and putting plans
in place to ensure he would be able to get enough
money together to be able to afford the course,
he was informed at the end of the half-hour
appraisal that he would not be offered an oppor-
tunity to participate.

It hadn't gone that badly, he thought – the
panel had shared a smile between them while he
spoke passionately of his love for the theatre –,
but the chief judge explained to him warmly that
this was a masterclass for *dramatic* acting, not
comedic acting. He'd not mentioned comedy
even once in the interview, and the monologue he
had given was notoriously devastating. They must
have been hysterical after a long day of interviews, he thought, remembering the way they had
laughed wildly when his cap fell off the back of
his head while he was walking dejectedly out of
the door.

He had seen Marianne R. in a whole host of
productions, and greatly admired her often digni-
fied and subtle performances. She'd played a
lawyer walking a tightrope between her career

and her morals. An applauding seal of a vice president to an egotistical head of state. The eater and spewer of red-hot blame as a spin doctor. A housewife constantly dancing around her wayward husband like an attention-seeking bear pawing the air. A parent jumping through every hoop to get their child into a local school. A musician always hanging in a swing bar waiting for fame – to name a few of his favourites.

He had to meet her. He had tired of improv and am-dram, private lessons, evening classes and auditions for walk-ons. He needed to know whether he would ever make it as an actor, and he knew that she would know, she would be able to see the real him, read him, tell him if his hard work really had been all for nothing. And he could imagine how exhilarating and inspiring it would be to meet her, the stories she would tell; she probably delighted in showing off! That would be quite the anecdote in future auditions. He pictured himself suavely reclining in his seat, nodding knowingly while she opened up about her life and work, a private performance, a special moment between master and apprentice.

He called her agent in Vienna and asked if he could get a meeting with her. 'Highly unlikely,' the man replied in a charming Turkish accent, 'but feel free to send her a letter, she likes those.' He wrote to the address he gave her, a hotel just outside of Glasgow, trying to keep it as brief and to the point as he could manage. *Could she spare a little time to discuss her craft with a desperately disillusioned emerging actor?* A few days later, he received a reply on a piece of headed notepaper. A large *Yes*, then a smaller *Date:, Time:, and Location:* and a very small *'Till then*. The signature was loopy and ornate.

She wanted to meet at Fylkir of Copenhagen on Newlands Road at noon. He sneakily swapped a shift directly with a woman he got on with from the same cleaning agency. All he had to do now was pick out the right jeans, the right shirt, the right bowtie.

He had always found men with thick, dark eyelashes very mysterious and brooding, and after studying countless head shots he was sure that some actors must surely wear a little makeup to intensify their features. This was the occasion to trial this enhancement. He had a tube of mascara he hid in a sock in a drawer that he had taken from the makeup bag of an aunt he sometimes visited in Rotterdam. He didn't go too often; she loved telling stories of him as an odd and clumsy and accident-prone child. She had different shades of mascara in her overflowing bag, and he chose the least dried up and claggy one. He unsheathed it from its sock, imagining he was a secret agent – it was actually a hidden knife or

95

a gun being pulled from its holster. He opened his eyes as wide as they would go, staring into the mirror with his mouth hanging ajar, and brushed up once and down once. He managed to poke himself in the left eye and reflexively clapped a hand over it.

He sighed with his whole body when he saw it was raining outside and gasped with his whole body when he saw the time. He slipped down the final few stairs on his way out of the tenement block, and then skidded through some sodden leaflets out on the wet pavement in his rush to the bus stop.

He dived into the café and shook his short limbs and head over the doormat. He saw a broad-shouldered figure wearing a purple silk scarf capping her head and tied at the base of her neck sitting at a small table near the back of the noisy, bright room. She had her hands folded patiently in front of her, and her eyes closed, a little smile on her dark red lips. Her fingers glinted with silver rings, and a menacingly tall folded umbrella was leaning against the table.

'Ms R., I'm Willem,' he panted. 'Sorry I'm a little late.'

'Not at all, I was just running through some lines in my head. It was very relaxing.'

He went to the coat rack to hang up his yellow raincoat, turning to smile apologetically to her as he did so. He turned in time to see it drop to the floor. He bent over to pick it up and knocked someone's chair with his backside.

'Excuse me,' he said, halfway between standing and squatting, miming hanging up the jacket to the older man he had butted.

While picking up the jacket and attempting to hang it again, he turned to apologise and dropped the jacket for a second time. This time, carefully bending his knees, he plucked up the jacket and carefully hung it on the hook. As he walked back over to Marianne R.'s table, he noticed she was staring at him wide-eyed.

'Let's have some cake!' she announced gleefully. 'Yes, good afternoon, we'll have two of those plump little doughnuts please. They have an apple filling, Willem! Two small glasses of ice-cold milk to drink, and espresso? Two espressos.'

While they waited, Willem smoothed out his damp CV on the table along with his list of questions and read them through quickly in his head, moving his lips, while Marianne R. watched him, smiling with composure. Before he could begin to go through them, she took the little pile and folded them away out of sight.

'Let's make some room, shall we.'

As the refreshments were laid out on the table she tittered and giggled, scrunching up her small, golden, wrinkly hands and shaking them about in anticipation.

'Oo, thank you, thank you!'

Willem noticed his lower back was starting to ache from sitting up so straight. He kept his head perfectly still and tried to only move his eyes.

'Ms R., I know how busy you are and I really appreciate your agreeing to see me. I wanted to ask…'

'Ah, you prefer sweetener to sugar?' she said more than asked, stirring honey into her milk.

'Um. I like the taste.'

He didn't particularly like the taste of sweetener. In fact, it felt like his actions were not his, and that someone else was making these stiffly restrained movements for him, like he was a marionette hanging from strings, or that his skin and every object on the table were covered in tiny, invisible fleas setting everything in motion.

'I see. Very good. Continue.'

'Is… that bad? That I chose sweetener?'

'No, no, no, please, carry on.'

'Yes. I wanted to talk to you about my future as an actor. I feel that I have great potential, but that no one can really see it.'

'These look fantastic,' she muttered, picking up a flattish doughnut topped with a dusting of sugar and eagerly biting into it.

He nervously stirred the powdered sweetener

98

into his espresso and knocked it back immediately, burning his mouth. He quickly raised
the glass of milk to his face, prodding the inside
of his nostril with the straw he'd failed to see.
He snorted, frothing the milk before yanking the
straw out of his nose, and the glass. He hoped
Marianne R. hadn't seen; she appeared to have
been chewing with her eyes closed.

'I've been trying to become an actor for a few
years now, on the side of a full-time job, and I
suppose I'm at a bit of a crossroads.'

'Have a doughnut, they're divine.'

He robotically picked up the plump,
pancake-like pastry and took a huge bite while
still talking.

'I had to meet you to see if – hm, it's very good,
thank you – if you had any advice for me.'

Marianne R. blew bubbles in her milk and
looked around the café without answering. She
put down her glass and licked her thumb to
pick up the leftover sugar on the plate, putting
her whole thumb with its long, maroon nail
into her mouth.

'Oh, excuse me, you have a fly, just there, on
your nose, allow me.'

Willem leant forward; the chair legs gave
a short screech against the floor as he accidently
bumped his palm into the actress's nose. She
looked quite shocked but smiled and gave an

embarrassed little cough, wiping her nose with her napkin.

'I'm sorry, I didn't mean to do that.'

Marianne R. balanced her face on her fist and surveyed him with amused brown eyes. She seemed very quiet and immature for such a serious, revered actress in her sixties; he guiltily felt a little disappointed. He tried to mirror her casual body language, settling his chin on his hand, but his palm was so sweaty he slid off and had to quickly correct himself. He sat upright again.

'How do people respond to your acting?' Marianne R. asked, cocking her head.

'How do they respond? As in, do they like it?'

'I mean, how do they respond? Do they respond in the way you would like them to respond?' She took two long nips of her espresso.

'Well. I would say that I'm not taken seriously as an actor. People don't seem to care about openly laughing at me, in fact. No matter what I do, people just stare at me, smiling. Always smiling! They say I have "a naïve charm" or "a childlike quality". Everything I go for I'm told I'm not right for it. I've been called "a natural" so many times, but "a natural" what?'

She didn't say anything. She looked at him, a bold smile fixed on her face, shaking her head a little. He took this to signify that he had exhausted her patience.

The waiter came by and laid down their bill paperclipped to a Tarot card.

'Ah, Death!' Marianne R. beamed, sliding it towards Willem like another pastry.

He looked distressed and confused.

'*Rebirth*, Willem!'

'Let me get the bill, it's the least I can do after you've listened to me babbling on for so long,' Willem said urgently.

His hand knocked over the small glass vase between them, the single red carnation landed on the table and a spray of water studded the black silk robe Marianne R. was wearing.

She rose up, then began to tremble. Her eyes and mouth were puckered closed and tears formed in her crinkled eyes. She placed both hands flat on the table and bent slightly at the waist, making gulping noises.

Willem jumped up, knocking his knee painfully on the table and hugging it to himself, standing on one leg. He asked Marianne R. if she was alright, he was so sorry, was she unwell?

She wiped her eyes with the back of her hand, pinched her headscarf back down her forehead a little, took a few breaths, 'Delightful. Delightful!' She looked at her watch and could see an imminent exit in her future.

'Darling, you're an absolute riot,' she shrieked, gripping his head with both cold hands and kissing him on both cheeks, *mm-wah*, *mm-wah*. 'You have absolutely nothing to worry about. Please, don't let *anyone* take you seriously!' she chided, picking up her umbrella and round, black purse with his crumbled papers sticking out of it. She artfully laid down a note to cover the bill, patted his CV, chuckled her way out of the held-open door, trailed a waving hand behind her and climbed straight into a waiting car.

And she was gone. He flopped back down into his chair and watched the car drive off. He turned his head away from the door and was drawn to his reflection in the back of the brushed chrome coffee machine.

His lips pink and sore from the hot coffee, cheeks flushed with the imprint of Marianne R.'s lipstick and streaked with powdered sugar, his nose red from the cold, bluish mascara blotchy around his eyes.

He screwed up his face and stuck out his tongue, just to see if he liked it.

The Amnesty

Below you will find extracted responses from the writings of PERSON A *and* PERSON B. PERSON A *is an anonymous voluntary respondent to the first Amnesty on Sexism survey sent by the government to every woman and girl over the age of fifteen.* PERSON B *is an unidentified male whose diary entries on the subject of the Amnesty were saved in the Drafts folder of their private email account and donated as data for research by the Lynx media corporation after liquidation.*

While reading the below texts, consider:

1 *Whose argument you find the most persuasive;*
2 *What* PERSON A *and* PERSON B *might be hiding;*
3 *Whether things have changed;*
4 *Other questions you would have liked to have asked* PERSON A *and* PERSON B *and how you think they would have answered them;*
5 *Whether this relates to your own experiences.*

*Do you think having an amnesty
is a good idea?*

'Amnesty' comes from the same stem as 'amnesia',
which strikes me as odd in this case as once all
this is out it's not like it's going to be forgotten?
Like, we'll receive a notice of receipt and a thank
you and then we'll forget about the inconvenience
and the fact that most men – but not all men
– are unworthy of being called human.

When I got to the office, I decided to start filling
out this form. You've given us a lot of pages.

I started thinking about the two on the train.
I couldn't get them out of my head. I stared them
both down on the tube, that homogenous landscape they formed. They all dress the same.

Two men sitting next to each other at one end
of the carriage. There are four main categories:
boys, young men, men, old men. One was very
young, not boyish, but certainly below twenty
and was wearing knee-length shorts and a short-
sleeved top, both in matching silk or chiffon, pure
cream. His hair was also dyed darker than suited
his complexion. He wore leather slip-on shoes,
which encased his feet like rounded slippers. He
looked uncomfortable, perhaps regretting having
so much flesh on show, and he must have been
cold, thick hairs were fuzzing the line of his arms
and his legs.

Who first discovered that seeing a peak of a man's stomach evoked a warm feeling in women? That the more of the stomach he felt a woman see, the more he wanted to give it away? Most keep it completely covered, others are more daring, using mesh or lace. When did that accidental thrill become expected, asked for, demanded, sought out, thought out, manipulated, used for a certain power against us women?

The older boy was probably sixty and completely pointless, stylish in a heavy black sack that went just below the knee, thin white stockings, white slippers to try and promote the elegant line of his bag-of-bones feet. A black shawl of the same heavy black felt was pressed to his chest with his gloved hand. The other glove, red as arteries, poked out of his pocket. His shiny bald head made him look vulnerable. He was wearing powder on his face and a little eyeliner. He was probably the director of a company, shunted in to fill a largely silent role, and would probably get flustered and stroppy in the mornings and evenings. I stared at the young boy and imagined touching the wound of his breastless chest, the humiliating growth packed into super-soft underwear. I thought about summertime when women get on the tube shirtless: a man would always grit his teeth and remove his own shirt in defiance, but would always be shouted out of the carriage, or things could get nasty if women dared to touch him, laughing throatily.

They practically ruined my day because I couldn't stop thinking about how utterly inadequate they both were to me. I went over to them, hung my bag off the shoulder of the young one and put my wide-brimmed hat on his head, and lay my briefcase on the lap of the old limp thing, popped it open, took out my newspaper and started reading it, silently defying either of them to look at me.

(PERSON B)   As I haven't been asked to write anything I'm going to open this non-email with a question. When we look up 'how to introduce a cat to living with a dog', what is it we are actually doing? Trying to avoid a violent confrontation between the two animals? Hoping to see examples of ways to approach the meeting in order that neither of the animals gets distressed or suffers long-term trauma? It could be that we're trying to understand the animals more deeply and see if such a combination of animals and this kind of situation are recommended, or even possible, right?

Whatever the motivations are for such research, what we are actually doing is being comforted by text. If the thing we fear and don't understand is written down, then it can be studied. It is an answer. A fear with an answer, logical or otherwise, cannot be so fearsome. We write about what has happened, could happen, and is happening, to make us feel like we have a plan for the future – that when the time comes, we know what we must do.

In truth, one cannot pin down how x feels about y and vice versa and know why it is they feel that way, how they will act, what they will do, what they are capable of, even if they tell you everything.

One thing is certain – and we know this without any report drawn up from this survey: the hatred of men is epidemic and the centres for the treatment of misandry are full. And I don't know if asking women to write what they think about men in some confidential survey makes me feel safer. I feel like I can hear a million marks being made on a million pages, and it feels like laughter filling the void we're being forced to guard.

I honestly think that this amnesty on private fantasies, thoughts and fears has made the situation worse. I don't know. It's possibly just brought everything out into the open. The endless arguments in parliament, the heated panel discussions, the polarised newspaper articles, the sour conversations down the pub, attacks in the street and in public places on the rise. I go to bed, but I don't sleep. Yet I feel compelled to write.

I've been working two full-time jobs to get
by since I had to leave teaching. During the day
I work in a café, in the evenings I renovate old
houses. From 7 a.m. until 3 p.m. I froth milk,
toast sandwiches, scrub toilets, wipe tables; then
I walk across town to the… I suppose you'd call
it a mansion? Get there for 4 p.m. and leave
around midnight. Walking is the only time I have
to think, but I choose not to; I pay attention to
walking not too fast, not too slow. Sometimes,
if I feel anxious, I pay the twenty-five pounds to
use the smooth chrome super-shuttle that takes
me from the building job straight to my door
in under a minute. I can barely afford it, even once
a month. I often think of those men that can't
ever afford it.

Every day for the last six months I've made
an extra-hot latte for a woman who never looks
me in the eye and is careful to always touch
my hand for too long when I hand her the cup.
It's the same woman whose house I've been
renovating and reinforcing with concrete and
bullet-proof glass for the last three months, and
she's never acknowledged this. Maybe she hasn't
noticed. I noticed the pale green amnesty forms
in her bag last week, already partially filled out,
and the few words I saw, and the ruthless heavy
crossing out, made me feel sick.

(PERSON A)   *Do you think there is a fundamental problem with men?*

Men don't get to bleed pith every month, they are just shrivelled and ageing permanently. Shame and vulnerability and responsibility from when, as the Bible says, the baby chose the woman for the first pregnancy, and it has never gone any other way. The primal denial of the receptacle. To father something dictated repulsion, an escape, a near miss. To mother something was to be the saviour, to be the everything. A child should only be allowed to see their father with female super-vision, just in case they're jealous of the mother's status as the chosen one, or in case they influence the child too much. In my opinion.

(PERSON B)   When my partner and I were as-signed a son in the adoption lottery after nine years of waiting to reach the minimum fathering age of forty, someone left a card of condolence in my ruck-sack and a camouflage romper that said 'I'm a little trooper' with a picture of a soldier's helmet on it.

(PERSON A)   *Do you think men are weak?*

When I give my talks at female empowerment conferences I like telling the story I call 'My

Forty-Year-Old-Virgin Thinks of My Kiss'. It had taken so long to get enough interest out of myself for this boy in his forties – so coy and silent, he took convincing in tiny steps. Finally I took off his clothes and realised that I had not changed the way I regarded him or any object associated with him; he received the same lack of real attention as the door I had opened, the floor I had trodden on, the lightbulb at the moment of combustion. I didn't think of his self-consciousness and started undressing once he was wholly naked, slightly curled on the bed looking up at me while I talked about how tired I was after a long day, all without any real thought. How I gripped his pinned-back arms and stared. I have this trick where boys think I've kissed them. The follow-up messages I would never reply to would peg a story up on the kiss as the remarkable proof of some hopeful impression, when I in fact never kiss. They just think I must have, after all the things I do to them. Everyone laughs at this point.

(PERSON B)   Even though I've been working on her house and giving her coffees every day, every evening I feel like I'm invisible to her, though she absolutely must know I exist as a unified entity.

She passed me in the street once, taking me by surprise and, without stopping moving, asked if I had seen her email. She half heard my answer that I thought she'd mistaken me for someone else, said pardon, acknowledged the pronunciation of the first letter with a lolling double nod and set off on the other foot, not once looking at me but gripping my upper arm roughly for not even a full moment. I might not have had a face.

She didn't speak to the new project manager for a week because he had addressed her using her first name the first day she was on site. It was obvious that she was older than him, and in the hierarchy pyramid in the staff office (nine steps high) he was one level below her – one plus one equals title and surname.

She enters conversations as if she had started them and everyone else was interrupting her. It didn't even really matter what the conversation was: she says thank you twice as loud, pours out sarcasm and unfunny jokes constantly. No one would expect her to react in any way other than with a single word or a long monologue-like point without taking a breath.

(PERSON A)   *Have you ever harassed a man in the street?*

I suppose you mean, have I ever tried to hook up with a man in the street? Sure, this happened this morning:

'Hey, where are you going?'

'Sorry, I don't know you.'

'I know you don't. Where are you going?'

'I'm not telling you.'

'Why not?'

'Bye,' and he tried to walk faster, hopefully upset, his bent shoulders protecting the back of his neck. I think I shouted 'Pathetic dick!' at him because he was rude. There's nothing worse than bad manners.

(PERSON B)   Only wealthy men can afford to act like women; they can do theatrical sighs, ask endless questions. Their parents allowed them to forget the general status of men in the world. They're making fools of themselves. What a childish make-believe world they live in while all us other men laugh furiously and hysterically in the wake of their stiff, punctuated walks. Some men are louder: laugh longer and louder, agree louder and with repetition. Unnecessarily, super-fluously compensating for conversations not in their abilities to manage. Introduce, hold up. Even if they started, they would probably give up halfway through and let a woman with no better point than theirs take over. What's the point? Fuck, what am I saying.

The whole world exists so that women can receive leisure and comfort and have all their

ideas put through, chosen only because there's
no other option, creating more pleasure-receivers
and more pleasure-givers, and if that were to
change, no decisions would ever be made, right,
no one would know who was giving and who
was receiving, nothing could be agreed upon,
every sexual session would end in the melancholy
of the unachievable and resentment at over-sharing.
Winner-loser, giver-taker, upper-lower. To have
been born a woman, though, would have been a
miserable fate.

(PERSON A)   *Can you control yourself
around men?*

Walked to the cusp of a boy's personal space as
we went down the stairs into the underground and
barked 'move' so loudly and so forcefully I only
realised what the noise was a beat after I'd done
it. I walked in a curve to a young man waiting
against the station wall and said something to him,
turning my back on him straight after and stood
barely an inch from his folded face to look at my
phone with his confused breath on my neck.

(PERSON B)   There are low stools in all shops
because it is a gaze of power to look up at someone, as if from hell, or as if from the body, rather

than from some non-existent holy being from above in stores and coffee shops. I always have to serve from a raised step so the customer will have to force themselves to strain to look upon the horror of me and to give them the power, to form a contract in performance that there would be no rudeness, purely a transaction. Many men far chirpier than me give the impression that they enjoy working in such places; they are brazen, flirtatious, a boldness that soon fades once they are back out in the street after their shift has ended, surrounded by women about their shoulders, looking up at heart height, making them feel conscious of their flat chest and twitching penis.

When I end my shift, I feel exposed, high and easy to topple. When I'm looked at, I feel like hot meat. I've recently transitioned to wearing a shawl over my shoulders that goes down to my ankles, even though I feel hot and like the look of my body in my bedroom mirror.

Most women wear tights and leotards, or one-pieces, and show everything, with gloves and short, long or no hair, wire headdresses and shoulder extenders that would stick in your exposed skin, like getting prodded by the prongs of an umbrella. They're well-exercised, show off their vocal coaching, endless resources, everything sized for them, smaller than a man could bear as their cumbersome, overlarge bodies spill over the edges of the toilet seat, over the end of the bed, squeezed in the bath, in the lift. Looking down and away like young children.

After a certain time, the body begins to die. The perfect moment runs for a second, and then suddenly clothes appear like the cover to protect the shame of a corpse. Clothes get newer, but the body gets older and older; clothes become ugly, like a joke or a disguise. I am disguised as youth and jealous of the truly young.

(PERSON A)   *Have you ever attacked a man?*

Once the house is ready everything will be normal again. I like walking from town out to the gated community with the long, curving driveway, where the house is half hidden behind a labyrinth of hedges. I was about twenty minutes away, strolling along, whistling, when I saw a hot man walking in the middle of the street with his head down. I clapped my hands together, rubbed them for luck, walked up to him and put my hands on both his shoulders.

'Hey, hey, it's OK, how about you come home with me?'

He opened his sleepy blue eyes wide and stepped back and said, I couldn't believe it:

'What the fuck did you say to me?'

117

I was gobsmacked to be honest.

'Look, cock, how much? Stop messing me about otherwise you'll lose your chance.'

I could see people looking, I smiled and opened my arms out wide.

'Who do you think you are? I'm on my way to work and you think you can talk to me like that? It's pathetic!' he shouted, almost laughing as he shoved me in the chest.

I started slapping him on his arms and legs, punched him in the face, grunted at him, leant over and stared at his crotch grunting and snuffling, then carried on walking.

(PERSON B)   She had stormed in without saying a word. She was obviously in a bad mood. I was painting a low part of the coving.

She walked in, spat on the concrete floor, threw her coat over a stack of boxes and stood in the corner of the room facing out, shouting her questions and replies from her vantage point. She pulled up her shirt to scratch her chest.

She started lifting and chucking half bags of unmixed cement into another corner, and then stopped and looked at me.

'This is more your job really, isn't it hulk?'

I looked down and across from the stepladder and paused for a second.

'Well, I'm painting right now, Sir, maybe I could do it tomorrow…'

'I can't hear what you're saying, mutt, speak up.'

The other men looked at me.

I opened my mouth, closed it, lay the brush across the rim of the pot and descended the three steps very carefully.

She approached me quickly, she was really close all of a sudden. I half turned my face towards her while wiping my hands and felt her spit with its sour milky coffee tang land warm then cold on my eyelid, cheek and neck.

(PERSON A)   *Do you think girls and boys should mix?*

I've told the girls to stop hanging out with boys so much; it will dumb them down, weaken their future networks and make them less appealing. They got back from a band practice – two boys with them – and I said while pouring them orange juice that it wasn't normal for boys to play in bands; maybe an all-boy band – that would be cute. When I told them, they looked at each other and laughed and each hugged one another like they were related. They'll grow out of it once the hormones kick in.

(PERSON B)   My six-year-old son came home today and said that at school they held their own amnesty and I asked how he felt about it and he said, 'Being good friends is more important than stuff like that dada.'

(PERSON A)   *Should the age of participation for the amnesty have been lowered to thirteen?*

My thirteen-year-old daughter came home today and said that at school they held their own amnesty and I asked what she said about boys and she said, 'Everyone is different and an individual with different strengths and weaknesses and we shouldn't place expectations on anyone or treat people differently because of their role in reproduction or resort to biological essentialism to classify somebody.'

They're not being prepared for real life.

(PERSON B)   When I started writing these emails, I wanted to send them to someone in the temporarily instated amnesty department. Or to her. To her? I opened a new email and in an apoplectic hurry started typing 'Women', but instead of beginning to type in the body of the email the ticking cursor was in the recipient space, where what

I wrote was flagged up as an invalid addressee:

women x

To write an email to all women. I kept writing.
I spent over an hour editing it. I pressed send
in a rush of excitement. It warned me about doing
this, refusing to comply. I guessed a possible
extension:

women@women.com x

I clicked send, knowing it would return moments
later, but I did not feel disheartened. I carried
on writing them regardless. They can just sit here
in my drafts folder, growing in the dark, waiting
for their time to come.

(PERSON A)   *What is the future of gender relations?*

I came downstairs last night to get a glass of
water and found my eldest daughter reading my
amnesty forms in the glow of the open fridge. She
looked up at me, but she didn't seem inquisitive
or proud or afraid. The look she gave me was
mysterious and I couldn't explain it. I felt stifled,
small in a bad way, and I didn't have any explana-
tion for her expression.

She offered to let me read her forms tonight. I said to her, but I suppose more to the TV: 'Four words, Frances – old, dog, new, tricks.'

Discuss in your groups.

Notes:

The Binding Reach
After Wikipedia

I own Joe Bethancourt's first banjo, the old
S.S. Stewart his grandfather gave him at the age
of nine in Phoenix. I am Bethancourt's nephew,
Tom Purtill. Bethancourt picked up the banjo after
hearing his grandmother, C.H. Burnett, play the
fiddle. I've never played the banjo, except strum-
ming at his in time with the lunging steps of
Li Ling the Chinese shot-putter during his winning throw in Osaka across my television screen
in 2007. Scratching at the strings was a remote
distraction, something to ride on my mental
hopes that he would somehow fall or fail. He got
19.38 metres.

Back then, as I had done for many years
previously, I enjoyed driving around making
faces at oncoming drivers, stretched wide-eyed
smiles, dramatic and painful frowns, screaming
mouths, that kind of thing. I didn't bother
doing this on my way into college, Bryn Mawr.
I was always feeling drained of mischief in the
mornings and early afternoons after nights away
in the city minutely adding to the spreading
tattoo on my stomach at Roy Chamb's, or laying
around on my girlfriend's bathroom floor reading
out-of-date photography magazines while she
had four-hour baths. My mother was from Abra
de Ilog in Occidental Mindoro. She left to study
the genus of moth called Melgona, in spite of
her simple family's assurances that this would

only end in trouble. Within months of landing in America she starred in Maxwell Anderson's play *Valley Forge*, playing George Washington's wife. She could play any nationality, so long as she didn't have many lines. It was her particularly sublime features, beautiful in how striking she was, that detracted from a question of nation.

Only mother could help me when I murdered Stefan Ekberg. Murdered him from my past. Stefan had returned from the motorcycle speed-way championships in Great Britain having won in the Premier League that season. He came to me – me in my shabby smooth suit and flat shoes, him in his bad skin – to tell me he was leaving me for Herbert Kraus's grandson, Thomas. Mother and I took this as a personal familial insult, us being cousins of the Oehler Brothers, the true masters of Nietzschean scholarship, unlike the disgraced Herbert Kraus, a weak-minded *jus synthétiseur*. I completed my studies full of rage and insecurity, and became Junior Head of Remote Surgery at the Institute of Advanced Studies at Princeton, New Jersey. To think I'd gone into telepresence purely because of the Lindbergh Operation, the first remote surgical procedure, which I read about in the newspaper. Dr Jacques Marescaux removed the gallbladder of a man in Strasbourg from New York in 2001.

I kept a copy of the opera – or rather *dramma per musica* – *Scanderbeg* in the second drawer of my desk. I was consumed by how much the picture of Vivaldi on the inside cover looked like both my old lover and my mother. I couldn't read the actual opera very well. Vivaldi's white hair didn't so much grow from or seem even attached to his scalp, but sat on top in obvious wig status, floating and emitting a yellow-grey light from his young-man-old-woman face.

My first operation would be on Adam Silverman. Silverman. Silverman. It wasn't successful; this silvery man, he went the colour of money. Someone in Atlanta brought him back to life, mistaking my smile on the video screen for mild hysteria at my remote robotic hands' subtle fuck-up. I kissed my own hands post-op. I'd read up on this man. He'd written an opera, *Korczak's Orphans*, found on the same shelf I'd accidently come across *Scanderbeg*. Janusz Korczak, or Henryk Goldszmit, supervised orphans in the Warsaw ghetto; his death march with the two hundred young Jews was seen by Władysław Szpilman himself. An opera for a martyr-Jew? And a *Theaterstück* inspired by Nabokov's *Lolita*? I shook my head in sorrow.

Four months after the operation, Adam Silverman stood in the foyer of my apartment building, seven floors below me, while I, none

the wiser, watched *The White Tower*, drawn
in by Alida Valli, counting out her ancestry
in tears, and Adam Silverman, the silvery man,
was coming up.

Due Process

When I asked my sister for a divorce ten years ago, she screwed up her eyes and smiled. The light from the window was blasting her in the face. She probably couldn't see how determined and tired I was. *What are you talking about? You don't mean it.* I made myself keep standing at the side of her workbench where she was scratching away at scraperboard surrounded by photos of ruined castles for reference, the apprentices shuffling about around us. *We're the Craiggowie Sisters. We always have been. Hazel. Lilian. Hazeland-Liliancraig-gowie.* She knew that she had done it this time, she was laughing too openly.

She had got back half an hour before I did after another dismal meeting with a gallery. She'd got bored of compromising, walked out, got on her motorbike and come straight back to the studio. We'd just won that big award at the time and I had the feeling that this would be the end of us. After we'd said our thank yous and were smoothing down the backs of our black satin suit and peach chiffon dress to seat ourselves at our table with the rest of the gang she said what I thought she might over the applause: *Now we can start the production line.* She said it just as I was about to shout 'A new start!' into the abyss of the commotion.

She was stubborn. If anyone questioned her conception of an exhibition, she would either

131

clam up and shut down, fold her arms and stare
into a corner, or flip out, throw notebooks, knock
over chairs, shout that they were questioning
her integrity. It wasn't the first time that I thought
what she was saying was without substance,
another pitch about commenting on large corpo-
rations and capitalism to an engorged gallery, but
this time there was a funny kind of shame at being
associated with her, even and especially after all
these years. I repeated what I had just said: that it
was time to separate, and to make it official. It
was for the good of both of us, and, more importantly, the work. One of the apprentices tried to
make their eyes look out the back of their head by
tilting their chin towards us slightly.

We'd divorced our parents when we were
fourteen, and with such fantastic results. We both
moved out, broke all contact with Phil and Sue
Craiggowie, changed our names from Amy and
Emily and went on to lead independent, successful lives the way we wanted – but always together.
Living, working, eating, socialising together.
Working on the same projects, the same subjects.
Seeing and sleeping with the same people, washing together, sometimes sleeping in the same
bed. Applying for the same individual artists'
grants and awards, being unanimous when judging prizes. Critiquing everything the other did,
making alterations to each other's work so that it

would 'fit'. It had to recognisably be a Craiggowie. Make it a Craiggowie!

She kept smiling and looking at me. *Sure. Let's talk about it later.*

I said that things wouldn't change much. We could still work together, but maybe we should think about living apart. She seemed very calm, but then so was I. When we left our parents, who sobbed and screamed at us, we smiled serenely. We, of course, were leaving the past behind and moving on from our false, stagnated lives.

We continued to live together while I looked for another house with or next to a studio.

After dinner she would do the washing-up and say *just popping out* and wouldn't be back for an hour or two. I assumed that it was to work on something in private in the studio next door, or to avoid me.

One day I went into her side of the house to ask her about a delivery of enamel paint coming in that afternoon. The floor in the bathroom was wet, she must have showered recently.

I went into her bedroom expecting her to be there, but she wasn't. I noticed that her low coffee table had been pushed to the side, leaving an expanse of carpet. There was the smell of sweat hanging in the air. Something green caught my eye on her desk. It was a stack of photos of gardens. I wondered if they were someone else's, but

I recognised both of our neighbour's yards, and the large garden over the back of the fence at the bottom of ours.

Though our final dinners in the house had become silent, as if our cutting, chewing and swallowing was the process for a new piece of sculpture in the workshop, I asked her about the photos.

Is this what you've been doing? Spying on people?

There weren't ever any people in them, mind. They didn't include windows or back doors, they were just of the gardens, all taken in dulling daylight.

Lilian said it was for a new project, but she couldn't tell me what.

Oh, something to do with corners, back corners of gardens, the shadowy parts of them, how they remain the same all year round.

I hadn't noticed that all the gardens in the photos had patios. I also didn't notice that there wasn't a photo of our garden. We had a patio.

She told me that all would be revealed tomorrow.

The photos were all out on the dining room table when the police came a week after she'd reported me missing.

What are these? Have you been going in people's gardens, Miss? What for?

You're not looking hard enough, Lilian stated. It didn't sound like an accusation.

Miss Craiggowie, we've been questioning local residents and making searches, please don't trespass on other people's property. There's every possibility that your sister is still alive.

They talked about whether anyone had called making demands. If I'd been acting strangely recently. Any stalkers, superfans. If I had any former lovers who might want to hurt me. Whether I might have wanted to end my own life. Questions she'd already been asked so were easy to answer again.

If they'd looked around the garden properly on day one, they would have smelled the glue used to stick the moss to the newly laid, artfully aged paving stones, and maybe they would have investigated the muddy footprints made with brand new boots. They might have seen that the bird shit along the patio was still wet and too thick and that brushstrokes were clearly visible on the lichen overlapping the slabs. They could have even discovered that underneath a terracotta plant pot in the corner of the garden was a perfect miniature recreation of her stabbing and decapitating me in the hanger-sized pristine white basement of the studio.

She lured me down there to see what she'd been working on one evening after that dinner when she had a good mood that was off the scale.

She ballroom danced me through the work-shop, down the stairs, to the centre of the room, telling me that she was going to miss me when I was gone. I was kissing her face, laughing, tripping over myself, spinning, and then I was winded irreparably with a hiss. Those press-ups in her room had paid off.

After slipping me into a metal tank of prepared chemicals, she power-washed the tiles and colour-matched some of the paint from our recent works for bold splodges and collected up metal filings and wood splinters from our latest sculptures. She arranged everything over the floor with the careless precision only an artist possesses. Any sprays up the walls she added to with complimentary tones of guilt orange, squeal yellow, shame pink. The knife? Incorporated into our infamous blade chandelier, picked up and revealed the next day at the seafront gallery out of the city.

In the first year, the worth of the work in our name quadrupled. Lilian opened up a second, larger studio – The Craiggowie Sisters: Station B – and took on fifteen more full-time staff.

At the end of the second year, she had the Hazel Craiggowie Art Foundation created, where a small fraction of my unused income was donated to pay for students to go to art college.

Midway through the fifth year, she unpacked my notebooks and went through my sketchbooks, a minute spent on each page. Re-read interviews with me in art journals. Re-watched our hysterical appearance on that late-night art show on repeat. She started having a weird feeling, like, perhaps regret? Or, no, perhaps it was the twinge of the yawn of her lack of inspiration caused by viewing mine?

In year seven she was commissioned to write a book about me. She did meticulous research:

Hazel always thought that carpentry was the finest of all creative pursuits because of its closeness to nature, obviously now in its deadest, final form –

Hazel would have enjoyed the new trend for taxidermy –

At the opening of the retrospective, filled with the architecture sketches and suited-men paintings and recreated scenes from famous street protests in miniature, my bleached skeleton was arranged in my green work overalls standing at a blackboard with an illegible scrawl across it.

A number of visitors would mill around in the vicinity of me and mouth to their companion:

Her sister, they never found her you know, how sad, or, *Is that supposed to be Hazel? How crass*.

Lilian gave a little speech about how the Craiggowie Sisters were still going strong and that I had never really left, indicating me in the corner. There was some mild, low laughter at this. I loved Hazel for who she was, I know her inside and out. We'll always be a team.

I was a museum piece, surrounded by art that was being viewed and reviewed in the context of my absence, of my former, now permanent self. Art that meant nothing to me anymore.

If I still had a stomach, I would be sick to it from being so static. All the things I have not known and have not done and have not changed and have not become.

Lilian looked so happy. The heroine of her generation. Not our parents', but ours. *Craiggowian* had entered the dictionary that year. She had got to redraft the definition.

Lilian had maintained our trajectory, even when I had wanted to swerve.

Half-Learnt Lessons

Under the translucent sheet she suckles at sea air, awoken by strained voices calling everyone to prayer.

After padding to and through the door to the circular room beyond, Lindy keeps a constant waddle to her mother lying on the floor near the window. Her jangly shadow is pulled right across the cool terracotta tiles, moving angularly up the whitewashed wall. Though the apartment is blessed with much shade, the morning sunlight insists on being received through the three door-sized archways that lead onto the balcony. Both mother and daughter are messily reflected in the glass table, the gin bottle, the wine glass, and darkly in the framed landscape print hanging on the wall. The television, the brown Bakelite telephone, the black marble ashtray, they all witness a small dark figure against the light, conducting an invisible orchestra; really she's wiping her nose.

Lindy spreads both hot hands out across the belly of her mother and pushes a little, chatting at her. They were both only in their white cotton pants throughout this mock resuscitation. She clambered on her mother's legs, lying flat on her front, chest on hard knees, feet flapping near her mother's chin. She gabbled loudly, awkwardly rolled off, bones hitting tiles. Lindy noted that her mother had been replaced by a new yet familiar thing. For about half an hour she avoided the face by pulling at the fingers, dropping the whole hand like a bunch of keys onto her own lap from a height.

The idea that her mother was not sleeping, thinking, ill, or ignoring her blinked on and off in her head. This was serious, but incomprehensible. It marked a new time, a different routine. She had to *do* something. Lindy knew from somewhere that it was an evil thing to look upon the dead. Dragging her bed sheet by the corner over to her mother she chose to cover her face and chest, though her belly, knickered thighs and legs remained bare. It was somehow known that her mother would have to 'go away', because that was how it was.

Handfuls of her fat fingers had to be jammed into the scissor handles to give her a grip on them. Standing at the head of her mother's body, she bent stiffly over like a marionette and spread the length of its fine dark hair flat with her free, sticky hand. She jabbed the blades at the waves, which disturbed her. Then, at the darker streaks. Metal chinked on tiles, got caught and pulled out whole strands from the scalp. When a bird rattled the light swimming through the window she paused, unplugged her fingers from the scissors to let them breathe and throb. She sat cross-legged to her mother's right side and began awkwardly cutting lengthy locks away, to be lined up in a shiny dry row behind her. The cutting brought out the soft scent of her, especially when the bristled blunt ends were brushed against her nostrils and lips. She finished when she bored of it and her hand had numbed, leaving her mother's hair a disordered, greased, uneven thicket, full of hiding places and clearings. The children were calling for her. The scissors were discarded in the wood for later. Running back into the bedroom she dressed herself in yesterday's clothes, and without looking back at the body she left, barefooted.

When the cold had prickled her numb in the puddle-ditches behind the market, she climbed out, on the second try – a foot in the youngest bub's face – and ran home. She sang all the way up the staircase, squatting, squatting lower and pouncing up the final step to the landing with a solid bang. To open the door she hung off the handle and let it swing open a few inches; the wood on her face was rough, cool, momentarily absorbing. She licked it and squeezed the murky taste out of her tongue against her teeth. Lindy lowered herself grudgingly, planting damp dirty feet by the toes on the tiles. Already she could see the body, still there, in the window's tingling, moonlit insect stare. The silence of it bored her, or made her angry, or sad. Curling up against its side she drew the sheet over her, replacing a corner for her mother's bare belly. In the night she woke for a drink, and after dipping her hand in the old bathwater and licking her fingers she crouched and slid the cut hair across her arms, talking to it, laying it on her shoulder, piling it up eventually to release it in fluffy chunks off the balcony on the wind. It wouldn't talk back. Had she been forgotten? Was she here at all? Rashly, the point of the scissors pressed into the body's shoulder until the flesh gave, and then dropped. Sleeping would have to be done in the other room, in the wardrobe. The blouses that suddenly fell off their hangers atop her moppy head upset her into sudden screaming guilt, but soon warmed her with sanctuary.

* * *

Click. More shouting voices in a clean, well-lit studio on the screen. The picture was poor and overly orange. She talked back, but mostly sat open-mouthed and transfixed, squashing her neck in a comfortable way, quietly supervised. A feeling spread in the room, telling Lindy that she'd watched enough. Click.

She continued what she had started the day before by generously peppering the flesh with talcum powder, letting it drift into the parted mouth (for her teeth) then over the dulled green eyes so she could really sleep. Taking a cleaning

144

cloth from the kitchen she rubbed the body's skin
very gently, trying to mimic the way her mother
used to clean the kitchen table back at home. The
heat in the room was nauseating. She didn't mind
the hardened bread, which she sucked more than
ate. She had been drinking from the cooled drawn
bath for the second day, straining over the edge
and dipping her chin, mouth and nose into the
water, avoiding dead flies. But the water started
to taste wrong, so she tried standing on a chair
to drink from the sink, letting the water run.
It had been a struggle to turn the tap. A handful
of water nearly made it to the body's face, gluing
up the talc in droplet clumps. The dry bar of
soap she used both hands to chafe the powdery
arms with only made the motherly skin pinch
and wrinkle and twist. The soap slipped into the
ashtray before she scuttled back into the bedroom,
sneezing twice on the way.

Their shared holdall was still only half unpacked. She chose the cool, bitter-smelling men's
shaving foam. It spluttered a dribble of white
when she pressed the button with both hands flat
on its top. She took it to the body, her nose
streaming into her mouth, put the can on the floor
near the feet and stepped to depress the button
with her podgy foot, this time a thick scoop of
foam mounted a bigger foot. Smoothing it out and
up the leg, Lindy went *baaa* with a dribbling

mouth and decided to take some of the
cream back onto her own arm to feel its active
coolness. By the time she was finished she
was half-transformed into an alabaster sculptor,
transfigured into sadness, though it quickly
dried, and cracked, and crumbled onto the floor.
She took the glass and bottle, a small plastic
container and a half-full pack of cigarettes from
the table and put them on the body along with the
cheap purse from the expensive handbag in the
bedroom. The disgust for what she'd created
along with the hunger pangs hurried the ceremony.
A colouring book slid and settled on top of the
lot and, finally, she applied the reddest lipstick
from the holdall's wash bag as carefully as a
three-year-old can. A bald clown under a pile
of rubbish.

Once she'd drowned the room in perfume
she asked herself like her mother used to
– did she need to go? It finished with a round
of applause from the toilet. She thumbed a tacky
red button and ran off to the market, leaving
the door wide open. The television yawned into
being just as it slammed itself shut.

Gross Cravings

My ex-best friend recommended writing a pregnancy diary a long time ago, when she was
expecting her first baby. He must be seven years
old by now. Or around that. Could be nine.
I have to be honest, it didn't appeal. I spend all
day writing! Recipes and the lifestyle sauce they
swim in and the tiresome sprinkle of picture
caption seasoning, for both the new book AND
my bi-weekly column. And when would I even
find the time amidst the full-day photoshoots,
the late-night experiments and breakfast tastings,
the meetings with the publisher, the supper
clubs, the demonstrations at the height of festival
season, the mood boarding, the sourcing of ingredients, the snooping in the cookery sections of
bookshops? Then I wondered if it could become
an anchor in all this chaos. A record of both being
in the family way and this hectic period. I'm
determined to give it a go. And anyway – it'd
be nice to have something to pass on to the water-
melon seed when it's a spring lamb.

I wrote out a list of all the foods I'm no longer
allowed and pinned it to the fridge (with some
crap drawings o * #). I keep forgetting I have
to be wary of all of my favourite things: runny

149

eggs, too much tinned fish, blue cheese if unpas-
teurised, no G, and, apparently, because of
quinine, not even T. I was flicking through my
recipes and almost overnight they've become
poison – or proof of intent for committing infanti-
cide. If anything should happen, my ingredients
lists could be used as evidence against me, or at
least as proof of a certain reckless disposition,
a decadence, what kind of mother, etc. Reza said
I was being morbid and that no one would think
that when the book comes out.

WEEK 11

Well, I already seem to be failing at this diary!
Part of me didn't think Feta – what we've been
calling it – would stick around, but mainly work's
been full on. Knife to the Heart rejected half
the content I pitched and scrapped the photos
from last week's shoot at this morning's editorial
meeting. Not my editor to be fair – the mystery
big bosses who front the money for this tiny,
friendly-faced food publishing venture. Difficult
second book! I had to fight to keep Jo as the
photographer, but they might not be available
again for months and I'll be showing by then! I
haven't told anyone I'm pregnant yet. There's no
real rush. I know it wouldn't really change anything, though it doesn't really fit the feel of the

book. Reza suggested turning the book into one
for kids, or for busy parents, but I have no idea
where I would even start. The time my editor said
my just-out-of-uni-trying-to-get-my-shit-together
look was my USP keeps coming back to me like
ravioli rising to the surface of a pan. That was
four years ago. That first book came so easily. I
felt like I was in this magical state throughout the
whole project. All I remember was laughing,
cooking day and night through dark winter evenings – and the *blup blup* of raspberries bubbling
in a pan while it snowed outside. They teased me
about my sweaty grey face at the meeting, mistaking my morning sickness for a chic hangover.

WEEK 14

Though we've mainly been living on noodles
for years – if only all my greatest fans knew that
– I can't keep them down right now.
    See you on the other side noodles
~~~~~ < — noodles.
    Reza is getting more and more excited
about the baby by the day, it's all he talks about.
He's gone into dad-to-be mode. We have to be
prepared, he says, become more proactive. He's
considering applying to a private tutoring agency
for the period leading up to exam season on top
of his teaching. I don't know how he thinks he'll

be able to fit it in. 'I have to!' he shrugs. 'It'll be fine,' he says. But if he's busy working all the time, how will he help me when the baby comes – tell me that! He asked if I would consider being a private tutor too, for cooking, or journalism. 'Not really,' I replied, and he didn't push it. It should be the opposite of all this. It should be a chance to spend more time together, and with the new baby when it arrives. I have a helpless kind of feeling already, like I need to save us from a sorry fate of drudgery.

WEEK 16

I cancelled the Japan trip today. I had deluded myself into thinking it would all be OK and put off doing the maths, but it turns out I would be eight-and-a-half months pregnant when I went and it was supposed to be a six-week trip, so – goodbye big festival fee, goodbye catering that popstar's birthday, goodbye endorsement deal for that meat alternative, goodbye paid meet-and-greet at book one's Japanese launch, hello being charged a penalty of a percentage of the fees for the flights and hotels!! The thrill of irresponsibili-ty at going ahead with starting a family on Reza's teacher's salary and my piecemeal work as a food writer and one-woman caterer is starting to sour.

To try and put the disappointment about Japan

out of my head, I decided I would buy a new
bottle of perfume. I even went up to the assistant
at the counter in the department store on the high
street and asked for some recommendations. She
set down a selection of white scented strips on
a tray and one by one I wafted and sniffed them.
None of them felt very me – and then I felt my
eye drawn to a small teardrop-shaped bottle the
colour of olive oil. The woman shook her head.
It was very expensive, plus she would have to test
the PH of my skin before allowing me to try it.
I laughed self-consciously but agreed. No. I was
not a match. I was rated 'on the higher end of
acidic' – the perfume wouldn't function as it
should with my body as its host. It could be stress,
the woman offered, are you stressed? I told her I
was pregnant, could that have affected it? Ah yes,
mothers rarely qualified for this perfume, she
nodded sadly. I bought the same bottle of perfume
I always did.

WEEK 18

I was sitting on the top deck of a bus heading
home from an afternoon restaurant opening I had
no reason to be at on Friday, thinking about how
my advance for the book has almost dried up,
when I realised that I was staring at all the men
having premature knocking-off drinks in Bank

and Moorgate. I craned my neck and twisted around to watch them as we progressed along the street. All those men in their baby pink and baby blue shirts, pints in hand, barely a woman among them. I took the same bus route today on my way to find a few spices, and when the bus made its way along Threadneedle Street I saw a few men entering jewellery shops, or slipping into non-signposted restaurants, and a radical thought came into my mind: I could bleed one of these men dry.

I've seen the potential for this when catering private and corporate events with these kind of guys – they eat up the food, but eat me up more. They ask so many questions. Where did you get such a quirky fashion style? Do you hang out with arty types? How did you become so creative? Wasn't I afraid of my precarious situation? Did I make much money? And didn't I mind? They would be so easy to lure in. I love Reza, but – wouldn't it have been a smarter life choice to have married some old rich man? I rolled my eyes at myself and at anyone who had ever honestly had that thought. I had – such! – an impulse to get off the bus then and there though. And do what? I don't know. I felt an energy as we went through this part of the City in the honeyed light, and a pull as we turned a corner and out of the orbit of the Royal Exchange.

I went to visit Susie at the bike shop. We sat on the damp wooden bench outside in a break between bouts of drizzle and she quizzed me about Feta ('eurgh, don't call it that').

'Has mum been sending you long emails of great advice and typos?' – 'I bet Reza's been great, hasn't he?' – 'Are you going to be taking time off?' – 'Have you had any really weird, gross cravings?'

'A few weeks ago I could have killed for liquorice' – I confessed to her that I had eaten one black lace, and informed her about the new Finnish study that concluded it's bad for the baby's brain – 'but that faded and now I crave… money.'

'Oh yeah? I've heard about that. Pregnant women get a metallic taste in their mouth, don't they, like they've been sucking on pennies. Is that what you have?'

'No, I mean I crave money. A bank balance like a telephone number. I want to be around people with plummy accents who can barely pronounce words, their mouths are that twisted and rigid with entitlement. It's shameful really, but –'

'Yes, my love? You can tell me?'

'I've been walking around department stores and bathroom showrooms touching fabrics and running my hands over marble work surfaces.

I got a quote on a leather corner sofa that's the size of our whole living room, I have it written on the back of a card in my purse. And I've been looking up train times to Cambridge and Oxford.'

It all came pouring out of me like a rich custard. Then Susie's break was over. She gave me a long hug and rubbed my back. She put it down to the nesting instinct – I think she might be onto something.

WEEK 20

It's hard to cook when the bottom's fallen out of your stomach. My editor has sent two emails in a row asking after new – GOBSMACKING – recipes. I went out and bought a bag of random ingredients with my own dwindling money and laid them out in front of me on the kitchen table like the oversized pieces of an invisible chess opponent. Cognac for the queen, kirsch for the king, balsamic and sesame bishops, two pink grapefruit knights, a pound of sausage meat and a half pound of Roquefort for the rooks, obscure little tins and jars of things for some pawns. I sat and stared at them for twenty minutes with the oven pre-heating. I had to leave two other bags at the supermarket because I didn't have enough money. There must have been an idea in one of the bags I left behind. I know the inspiration's out there – it doesn't seem fair that I'm being denied it.

I cancelled the meeting I was supposed to
have with Knife to the Heart this afternoon and
went foraging in the dress I reserve for friends'
high-end weddings and my 'proper' makeup.
It was like I was in some kind of stupor. I walked
for hours around the City, stopping off at cafés
whenever I spotted a well-dressed man sitting
on his own.

There were men I was drawn to because of
their cleanliness and over-confidence, and others
because they overawed me with repulsion. The
uniforms have changed, I hadn't even thought of
that. The wealthiest tend to not wear ties anymore,
and if they're really wealthy they don't even wear
suits – more like trackie bottoms and baseball
caps nowadays. But I wasn't greedy. I just wanted
someone who wouldn't miss the money and knew
the places that would comfort and stimulate me.
I would explain to them after introducing myself
that I would like them to bless my child and to
place a hand on my stomach. Only a couple did
so, flattered. A few thought I wanted money.
One gave me a fifty-pound note to make me leave
him alone, and I fingered it in my pocket like a

good-luck charm as I continued on my way. I'm going to flatten it out nice and smooth while I wait for Reza. I can't wait to tell him all about my day.

WEEK 23

I went out hunting again today after a fortnight of misses. I've had intense encounters; I won't lay them all out here, it would take too long to explain, and I've gone over them all with Reza in detail already. This balance between attraction and disgust has been especially challenging. Just when I believe I'm ready to give myself up to one of these men, to seal the deal on a better and more secure life for my family, I leave in a hurry or I have to go throw up – I even puked over a Gary I met at Ye Olde Cheshire Cheese.

I felt so tired today I sat in Grind on Thread-needle Street and waited like a spider in a web. I made sure I was facing the door so I could see my prey, and so it could see me. Around eleven-thirty, an older man in a grey suit, white shirt, no tie, brown brogues, no socks, smoothed-back shoulder-length grey hair, came in holding the handle of a black leather satchel. He surveyed me with a look of surprise, cocking his head to one side as if he recognised me, then looked down clearing his throat and approached the counter to order.

I was sitting on the only table – high, small and

circular, surrounded by too-high stools with grey cushioned seats and low backs. It was a struggle to climb up into one when I got there around eight. While I was nursing my cold fresh mint tea and pointing my out-of-focus eyes at the white neon sign on the wall behind the counter that read 'CAN'T BUY ME LOVE', the man brought over his black coffee, sat opposite me and drew out his laptop to work. I didn't want to waste my time on someone who wasn't rich, and was about to move to the bar positioned at the window, when I noticed the scent he was wearing made my mouth water – it was citrusy but heavy with sandalwood. It had to be expensive. And I don't know anything about watches but his looked completely unique, personalised. If I looked closely enough, I could see the watch face was a scene of a man with a child over his knee, and with every strike of the second-hand his arm would sharply tick to spank the child's backside while the child's arms and legs twitched. The fabric of his tailored suit was an almost imperceptible mesh of a variety of colours, perfectly attuned to that silver grey, like a faultlessly balanced plate of food.

He caught my eye and asked if something was the matter – I must have been staring. I asked him straight up if he was wealthy, and he laughed and said, 'I think so, yes, but it's relative, isn't it?'

I told him my name, what I did for a living, and

that I didn't think he looked like a rich person. He asked if it was a compliment. I shrugged and tried to see if he made me feel nauseous by looking at him hard and taking a deep breath of him. No queasiness ensued.

'If you're looking for a job, I don't have anything going I'm afraid, and if you're after money I don't carry cash,' he said in a low and soft voice, as if he'd just whispered a sweet nothing to me, before taking a deep sip of his coffee. It was like this happened to him all the time.

I explained that I was looking for a benefactor because I was hungering after bettering mine and my family's situation. We deserved a raise. To not plateau, but to excel. I wanted my child to have security – not just the semblance of it, not just a make-do, make-believe life.

'What would be in it for me, other than a couple of homecooked meals?' he asked, closing his laptop and looking at me seriously.

I could be an interesting companion, his creative friend. I could go to events with him, I could stand next to him, be charming. But no funny business, it wouldn't be that kind of arrangement.

'I see. Like a sugar daddy?'

'No, no. A low-in-sugar daddy. An artificial sweetener.'

He thought about it for a moment, smiled, and then we shook on it.

Gaspar took me to a weird networking event
and I got to flex my credentials. All those uptight
weirdos lacking in self-awareness couldn't get
enough of me, they lapped it up. 'Ooo, Gaspar,
where did you meet your fascinating friend? I had
no idea you were so cultured! We should catch
up!' Then we went out to dinner at an incredible
restaurant in Maida Vale called Hunini. I had crab
and intensified tomato and we shared a carafe
(only a carafe!) of orange wine. He asked the
waitress if I could go through to the kitchen to
meet the chef – and it was Yōko Tawada!! I had
no idea she was the head chef there, and without
Gaspar I wouldn't have got to meet her or find
out that SHE HAD READ MY FIRST BOOK!!! AND
LIKED THE BRUNCH RECIPES!!! Chef Yōko said
to come by sometime for a chat. I wanted to tell
Reza but he was asleep when Gaspar's driver
dropped me off at the flat. He had left a present
for me in the kitchen, in one of those tacky
glittery bags you get in card shops – a little green
cooking apron. 'That won't fit me,' I said to
myself. I'm hilarious sometimes. Or maybe just
a little tipsy. Off to bed with me.

WEEK 27
None of my recipes taste right anymore. The

canapés, the granola, the cured fish. I don't know
what to do. My delivery date for the book is in
a few weeks. In fact, nothing tastes good anymore. I think my palate has completely changed.
Everything tastes grubby, or bitter, like I can taste
the sweat from someone who has handled the
ingredients before me. Last night I made the star
autumnal dish of oven-baked whole marrow
hollowed out and stuffed with pork mince and
garlic croutons and instead of the familiar
salivation in expectation at the melt-in-the-mouth
stringy green flesh, the tangy rich filling and the
juices dotted with oily suns begging to be mopped
up with sourdough, I gagged so hard my back
clicked. The wine – which I sipped before adding
it to the pork and onions – tasted like vinegar.

WEEK 28

After a few successful events and dinner parties
Gaspar has offered to pay me a salary to 'be me'.
I'm over the moon. I'm going to get a tidy sum in
my account every month for the foreseeable. I
told Reza, and he said he was pleased, but looked
exactly the opposite. 'It's philanthropy on a small
scale,' I said to him. 'I don't see the difference
between this and you tutoring posh kids.' He said
he did think it was a bit different. While walking
around an exhibition opening in Knightsbridge,

I asked Gaspar how he gets his money. I hadn't bothered asking before now, and he said that it would be best if I didn't know. When pressed he mumbled, 'Something with children, with babies.' Very admirable.

WEEK 29

I've figured it out. It's not the recipes, it's the ingredients – my palate has become more refined. I found this out the hard way.

I was slowly making my way down Eastcastle Road when I reached the Solstad Food Hall. I never usually go in there – only when I want to see how the other half live and to dare to ask for a sliver of some particularly exclusive cheese without making eye contact. It was raining. I felt dog tired. I went in through the brassy revolving doors and took a few steps across the peach floor veined with pistachio green and my senses began to hum. I took a deep breath in through my nose, saliva flooded my mouth. Every colour was saturated and distinct. A knife dully slicing through an eighty-five-quid game pie, encased in suede-textured pastry and encrusted with caramelised jelly the colour of oil, sounded like a bow passing over the strings of a cello.

I walked among gleaming counters, glinting boxes, decorative tins, feeling elated – and then I saw them. Yubari King melons. I'd read about them online. I bought a pair – as is the done thing, according to the salesman. I walked straight outside back into the rain and cracked one open on top of a stone bollard and gorged on it right there in the street. I have always cleared my plate, ever since I was a child, but it seemed uncouth to 'suck the bones'. I dropped huge pulpy clumps of it onto the pavement, and when I was done I wiped my mouth on the bottom of my baggy over-washed white t-shirt, showing the passers-by my stomach. Someone asked me if I was OK and if I needed help. No, I told them, I feel great. I looked glowing in my reflection in the shop windows as I carried on walking, swinging the bag containing the second melon as I went.

WEEK 31

Gaspar is letting me do interviews and press photos for the upcoming book at his apartment at the Barbican while he's at work. Our flat isn't right, and it would be too much work to get it right. I've been so tired lately, but his apartment gives me so much energy! Reza seemed put out when I told him. I reminded him that it's because of Gaspar that we were surviving. Gaspar pops round every now and then, just for a chat. I'll put my pencil to one side or turn off the hobs and sit

straight down on the stool in the kitchen still in
my apron and listen to him talk. Reza will give up
the other stool and do his marking in the bedroom
on weeknights, or go out for a walk if it's at the
weekend. Gaspar brings me wonderful gifts –
complex-smelling lotions and creams and sprays,
a comb with pearl inlay in the handle, black
velvet slippers, and sometimes he kisses me softly
and recklessly on my neck and behind my ear
while I speak. Reza walked in once while he was
kissing my bare shoulder, and Gaspar didn't stop,
and Reza didn't ask him to stop. Reza filled the
kettle, then leant against the counter and waited
for it to boil, Gaspar trailing kisses down my arm.
Then he made a round of tea for us all and left
the room again.

WEEK 32

I've been looking over the photos from the different shoots again. We purposely dotted the
evening-dinner-party-in-the-garden spread with
blurred fairy lights and tea lights to create a kind
of woozy ambience – the clothes are just blocks
of colour and the jewellery is also a collection
of out-of-focus blobs so you can't see how budget
it all is. My earrings and Reza's watch and my
friend Trixie's rings are all basically shiny plastic
to get a cheap glint. Our only perceptible features

are our teeth – we had to grimace at each other to make it look like we're smiling through the haze. It's just not good enough.

I made some calls and wrote some emails. A fashion brand has agreed to lend us their wares in return for credit in the photo captions. They couriered over some samples the same day. The material was so soft and lightweight – or luscious and heavyweight. They'll also pay for adjustments and alterations so it would all fit perfectly. The clothes all seemed utilitarian and like they could have been picked up in an army surplus or a catering wholesaler or a second-hand shop in a former industrial town, but they were actually all handmade from non-durable fabrics using anachronistic dyes with superior cuts and were remarkably expensive. The jeweller I found in town will pick out some items for me to try on later this afternoon.

WEEK 33

Today Reza blurted out to me completely out of the blue: 'I think you're enjoying it all a bit too much.' I looked up from reading a first edition of the English translation of *Feasts* by Rimple Kamra that Gaspar had given me as a present. I thought he was talking about the book. 'I didn't want to say that,' he quickly added, and then,

'I don't want to upset you, but I don't know if
the baby is an excuse somehow,' then something
about the doctor or the hospital! I told him that
he was being ungrateful and that because of
my sacrifice he didn't have to tutor in the evenings anymore, even though he still was out of
stubbornness. He asked me if I still loved him,
whether he was enough. I told him to let me
provide for the family in my own way, without
being shamed for it. Then he left for work. Gaspar
and I went to this beautiful old cinema with two
of his employees from work. Each group of four
gets their own double sofa and they serve you
dainty snacks in your seat!

WEEK 34

I went to meet Susie in the park – she childminds
on Tuesdays and Thursdays now for a bit of extra
money. It's a three-year-old girl called Yasmine.
Susie was preoccupied with entertaining Yasmine,
so I sat on the bench – practically crawled there
from the gates I was so shattered – and listened to
Susie chattering away at her two charges, sometimes in a baby voice for the girl, sometimes in
a grandmotherly tone for her sister. As she talked,
I looked at the child. I pictured my own baby at
this age with this entertaining and distinctive way
of being. If anything went wrong, if they got sad

or they had problems, I could afford to send them away to a private school or a private clinic. I wouldn't need to deal with it. That was a euphoric feeling, a get-out clause. We went and got ice cream from a greasy van. I threw my ninety-nine in the bin, flake and all.

Tonight was the big dinner party re-shoot at the flat. Gaspar's apartment doesn't have a garden – though he does have a view of the Barbican's lake and its foliage! – otherwise we would have done it at his.

Everything was set up and we started with some initial shots of the food – cold ruby beef with cavolo nero and mustard seeds, my rainbow 'slaw, nuggets of golden potatoes, rose-water sponge elevated with flecks of gold leaf (steam to be added in post-production), all made with the finest ingredients – and then some headshots in the kitchen for the inside cover in the self-creasing work shirt and the clinking necklace made of thin shards of silver that looked like scraps of foil.

Reza and a friend of his from the school were over an hour late because of a problem with the trains and I was nearly sick from the stress of prolonging the shoot. When he came through

168

the door he was drenched in sweat and wearing a black polo shirt and his five o'clock shadow was brimming over his jawline and I couldn't help but tell him quite insistently to go and have a shower and a shave and get changed into the mushroom-taupe jumpsuit. He didn't think I was being serious because 'no one will notice, I'm always out of focus in the pictures anyway, we can just get on with it' – but I was very serious and I think I sort of shouted at him, in front of the models I'd hired, to sort himself out. Everything had to be real, even if no one could see it or taste it. Reza reminded Jo that he didn't want any shots of his face.

Part way through the 'party', which felt a lot harder this time around, Gaspar arrived and joined us for the shoot. I made sure Jo got some nice close-ups of his fine hands and wrists holding his knife and fork over his emptying plate, and a few of him smiling across the table – there's some satisfying ones of him pinching the handle of an espresso cup.

As I was showing everyone to the door at around one in the morning, I heard something shattering. I thought Reza must have dropped a glass – it's not a dinner party if a glass doesn't get smashed, I thought happily to myself. Then there was another smash, and another. I rushed back through to the garden and Reza was pulling

the tablecloth in this slow, drawn-out pull, letting
the plates and glasses I'd hired fall onto the patio
in ones and twos. I didn't let myself get worked
up about it – my salary would cover what had
been broken.

I haven't written in the diary for a while, so
much has changed – obviously – in the last few
weeks. What happened of note today? I noticed
while sniffing herbs on the balcony that a bird
was mimicking the sound of the parcel courier's
gadget I sign to accept my daily packages. The
notice of a termination of contract with Knife
to the Heart came through the letterbox just after
ten, along with the new ceramics catalogue.

Got a text from Reza: *When will you be coming
home? I miss you so much. xxx*

I replied: *When the baby's here x* – as I've
said a hundred times! He knows I find it more
relaxing here.

Gaspar came home from work, washed his
hands and sat down at the smaller dining table,
the one with the fig-hued lacquer top. I carefully
set out the new paper-thin duck-egg-green
tinted crockery and the bronze-coloured cutlery.
He shook out one of the freshly ironed buttery
napkins with the red embroidery and laid it in his

170

lap. Then he did it again so it would lay more nicely – sharing a knowing look with me as he did so – and popped open the champagne like he does every night, right before we're served by the cook.

Apart From When

I only gained the ability to hear the town after I
    had moved away.
It has a certain background music that is inescapa-
    ble now whenever I come back.
It can give a stroll down a residential street a men-
    acing feel.
It's like a cry of wolf, but more a low whistle or
    hum.
People in the town started paying no heed to it a
    long time ago.
Or never really did.
There's the drone of aeroplanes toing and froing
    from the local airport.
(Oldest airport in the country. Art Deco. It's in an
    episode of *Poirot* – so says my Da every time
    it's mentioned.)
There's the hilarity of the seagulls, the two-tone
    foghorns from the harbour.
The long, thunderous *no* of lorries taking a
    shortcut through the high street to avoid the
    coast road.
And, if you're close enough, the sea's sore throat
    drawing in breath.
I can hear this soundtrack the moment the train
    doors open and I step down onto the platform.
I imagine the train has carried me up a long
    driveway from the city, where life goes on.
I like to pretend the town is a kind of rural opera
    house.

The station is the foyer.

The town is an everlasting performance, let's call it: *Apart From When.*

I once had a minor role that felt bigger than it was.

Now I get cheap tickets with a partially blocked view whenever I come to visit.

Out of choice.

But you cannot obscure its live score.

How I hadn't ever noticed it throughout my childhood –

Maybe it's the presence of these resonances that kept me alive during my teens.

Maybe it's the reason white noise makes me feel in an optimum state.

Could these unseen, far off sounds have kept my precise and local body in working order?

My body might have been in tune with the town back then.

A grey thread running from the church bells on the green to my aorta.

A green thread running from the train horns at the station to the crook of my arm.

It might have kept me ticking over, once, but nothing more.

I didn't die when I left.

In fact it was the opposite.

Things seem to happen more in the city.

I now think that this isn't necessarily the case.

I think it's more that everything seems more

changeable and precarious.

You're still allowed to be a romantic there.

There's a difference between being a romantic
and being stuck in your ways.

* * *

I'd been invited to give an exclusive reading of
a new story back in the town.

A lead role after all.

I didn't have a new story.

I haven't been able to write since the novel came
out.

Not a sausage.

Not a poem.

But it was a fundraiser for the coastguard.

And it was going to be at Sampson's Books.

It would make up for all the Sunday mornings I
came in late for my shift.

And I wanted to experience Shaun, my old boss,
within this new dynamic.

As an Author Coming to Read at the Shop.

And see how he is.

He's always the same.

I came down a day early to try and get something
down on paper.

I bought my Da's share of the small terraced
house on Pond Road that used to belong to a
grandparent I never met a while back.

With all the money from the first novel.

I wrote the new one in it, sealed up one winter.

The novel about the small American town and the large European metropolis.

(Not about a small, technically European town.)

The house feels like a sequence of small, round, cold shells linked together.

A dark hollow with a gas fire the size of a matchbox.

A television the size of a pocket mirror.

It's worth having just for the gate that shuts with a good, strong clunk.

A reliable catch.

And the long, thin, high window in the kitchen.

It frames a purpled hedge's brushy head and a bit of the creased white sky.

This window is like a box for a puppet show just about to begin, or just ended.

Set on the moors.

Wuthering Heights would be good.

It would have to be finger puppets.

Could I write a story after *Wuthering Heights*?

I didn't bother telling Da about the reading.

Or that I was coming down at all.

A flying visit is worse than no visit at all.

I reckoned.

I'll be back soon, I said to myself.

I booked in a drink with lovely Toby out of habit.

Sending text messages is too easy.

I didn't even remember sending the invite text.

It's always like having a drink with a video
  recording of Toby-from-school.
I ask him the same questions and he gives me
  the same answers.
But he is, and always will be, that reliable level
  of lovely.

Hello Shaun, I thought I'd pop in before tonight.

*Your reading's been moved to the new community
  centre. No, what do you call it. That new arts
  centre.*

What do you mean?

*It sold out. The woman doing the thing wanted
  to shift some more tickets.*

*But I was looking forward to it being here?
  At the shop?*

*It sold out! And there's a bigger bookshop in
  there anyway. They'll probably mark up the
  price by the way. We get to keep the booking
  fee. That's a consolation.*

*I didn't know. I'm sorry. Maybe I can get them to
  move it back?*

We've been promoting it off our own backs.
   Then I got a call this morning.

Will you still come?

I don't know, I don't know! I feel a bit pissed off
   about the whole thing now to tell you the truth.
   I have tickets for the air show, might pop down
   after closing with Charlie. Hello Derek, just
   the one?

Customers crowded around the counter and I left
   before I was recognised.
Would I have been recognised?
I might have been in the city.
There was only an upside-down smile and a nod
   with a raised hand when I said:

Seeyouinabitshaun!

I met Toby and his sister for a couple of drinks at
   The Anchor.
His handsomeness is wasted.
In any case mellowed by being best friends with
   his sibling.
I drank in the city fashion.
They were excited about the air show.
As if it was a normal thing to want to go to in your
   thirties.

They didn't bring up the reading.
I didn't mention it.
They left me by the roundabout.
Were they laughing?
I think it was happy laughter.
About that thing that happened to their friend
that time.
I must have wandered off in the opposite
direction to the house.
I remember the pebbles chattering as I bowled
down them on my backside.
The warning purr of the sea at night kept at bay
by sleeping children.
Rolling and unrolling in its anguish.
Its deeper, more beastly mother stirring the
bottom of the black curtain on the horizon.
I remember walking past Sampson's and seeing
multiples of my book swimming in the
window.
The carefully handwritten sign for the reading
had a plain computer printout stuck over it that
read 'MOVED TO BIGGER VENUE' with no
further information.
I noticed the chewing gum like limpets decaying
on the pavement for the first time.
The adverts in the newsagent's window all
seemed so obscene to me all of a sudden.
About animals and furniture and services.
I could still feel the bright tingle of thorn bushes

on my bare arms from the walk home in
    the morning.
And the gate connecting and reverberating
    through my hand.
And I had the memory of someone's wet face.
My last and first thought was that I still had no story.

I hung my khaki trousers over the wardrobe door
    while blow-drying my hair with the radio
    blaring.
A bit crumpled, the trousers, but that's what the
    fabric does.
The black roll-neck halter has a waffled texture.
Also good for masking rumples.
It was warm, but it would be too cold for shorts
    or a skirt later.
I turned off the cold stream of air and listened
    to the broiling voices coming from the white
    digital brick on the bedside table.
The music festival on the beach.
The farmers' market.
A reading by a big city writer who grew up locally.
The air show.
The amateur wrestling at the sports centre.
I had a lot to contend with.
Different kind of audience, I said out loud.
I must remember not to begrudge the local writers
    reading beyond their ten-minute allocation, I
    mentally noted.

A walk on the beach an hour before the reading.
That would be enjoyable and inspiring.
Something funny might happen.
The story could be a funny story.
I went near the home-time hour.
When the wind buffets sweatshirts, swimming
    trunks and jackets.
By the time I got there, there were just a few kids
    whose ages I still felt dormant within me.
They probably got bored at the festival and were
    getting drunk.
Their clothes were mismatched and their skin
    flush with sunburn.
I kept an eye on the one blossoming kid acting up.
He's sensual now, I agreed with myself, but to
    stay sensual he will have to leave.
Run, leave now while you still can, I muttered
    dramatically to myself like an old sage.
A soothsayer.

There was a choir of planes all around us.
What were they trying to say?
I could see them in the distance.
Hear them inside my chest.
They were crawling over the creamy blue sky.
And reflected in the windows of the private
    college for young men of the future.
The college beamed down onto the airfield and the
    looping dual carriageway from up on the hill.

The college looked yellow-gold and had a defined
    outline against the surrounding trees like a
    computer icon, an app.
It could be a collectible sticker straight out of a
    magazine – *Cathedral Weekly*.
To see the airfield I'd probably have to go up on
    the bridge that crosses the river.
The river that runs around the airfield and under
    the dual carriageway.
The arts centre is riverside anyway.
The town side of riverside.

I tried to pause on the bridge, but I couldn't.
It was already overcrowded.
Spectators kept tipping off the curb into the main
    road.
I kept walking instead of turning back around and
    entering the arts centre.
They won't be expecting me just yet, I shook my
    head.
I made it to the other side of the bridge and
    slowed down at the canal lock.
There were fewer people there.
A family dismounting their bikes appeared from
    the tight, quiet road that goes round the back of
    the airfield.

Is there a good view? Down at the end?

*Yes, really good, you just have to hop over the
    fence into the field and you can see the whole
    thing!*

Thanks.

Have to get this lot some ice-cream…

I should have turned back.
There were so many people on the bridge.
It would take at least twenty minutes to cross it.
You should have been there ten minutes ago, turn
    back, I thought to myself.
I put my sunglasses on my head and started
    walking down the road.

The trees couldn't block out the sound of the
    planes.
It sounded like they were gaining confidence.
Maybe I should ring the centre.
I didn't have a contact number.
I could ring Sampson's.
Shaun had probably closed up for the day.
The planes were too loud.
I remember putting my hands over my ears when
    we used to pay to get in to the air show.
It's too expensive now.
That's what Da says.

I mean, I could pay for my own ticket now.
And his.
I wonder if he went in the end.
It wouldn't be too much on his own.
I realised that he might have heard about the
reading tonight from the radio.
He always has the radio on.
I hadn't heard from him, so –
I did a pathetic run up the hill and climbed
awkwardly over the fence.
If any children were watching, they would
definitely know that I was an adult.
I sat in the field by a tree and watched the planes
grind against the sky.
Like metal jacks snatched up in a game of
Knucklebones.
The sun had bounced down behind the hill.
I unbuckled my hot leather rucksack and put on
my thin cardigan.
The sound would be unbearable at the air show
when we were kids.
It would make you feel nothing good.
Every time a plane flew low or tumbled
gracefully like a falling angel we would
point and jump.
We used to shout: *It's going to crash! It's going
to crash!*
We knew they never would, which is why we
did it.

It was make believe.

Willing a bit of danger to come to the town.

Wanting something, anything, to happen.

Nothing ever happens here, and never will.

It just carries on and I carry on coming back.

I felt like I was watching the trailers at a drive-in movie.

A stop motion animation for babies.

Then one of the planes started screaming.

Some people started screaming.

The plane was falling.

And it fell into the ground.

Then there was a flash and a belch of an explosion.

No, a *despair* of explosions.

I took out my notebook and a pen.

And made a start on telling the story of *Apart From When*.

I could do that now, now that the beginning had revealed itself in its end.

I should probably have waited for the flames to die down first, eh?

But I hope you enjoyed it.

Thank you all for coming.

And sorry again for being so late.

And for missing the other readings.

There wasn't time for a hello, so, hello! And goodbye!

I was hoping for a few more familiar faces, but, there you are.

We're fewer than we would have been, but, under
the circumstances –
I have to go now, but there are copies of my books
on the table.
And please give generously to this worthwhile
cause.

I'd like to thank Jess Chandler for publishing this collection and for being a bright and supportive force for myself and many other writers.

For listening and helping me find ways through, my eternal thanks go to Richard Phoenix.

I was *keeping it real* thanks to Rita Calvo.

For reading previous versions of these stories and giving me vital feedback, I'd like to thank Pardaad Chamsaz, Samuel Fisher, Jake Franklin and Will Rees.

For publishing and commissioning my short fiction over the years, including some of these stories, I'd like to extend my gratitude to Michael Caines, Jess Chandler, Rosie Day, Patrick Fry, Richard V. Hirst, Dominic Jaeckle, Joni Molla, Euan Monaghan, Cécile Menon, Suze Olbrich, Felix Petty, Philip Z. Serfaty, Daniella Shreir, Esther Strauß, Isabel Waidner, Brett Walsh, Flora A.X. Watters, Eley Williams, Heather Williams and Oliver Zarandi.

The alternative version of 'Town Called Distraction' was created in collaboration with Patrick Fisher.

Some of these stories previously appeared in *3:AM*, *Brixton Review of Books*, *Hotel*, *The Arrow Maker*, *Somesuch Stories*, *Podium*, *Funhouse*, *Ossian*, *Off Modern*, *PROTOTYPE 1*, as part of the pamphlet series *Détours* (Hotel/Les Fugitives), and on the records *Dreamlands* and *Deaths* by Sauna Youth (Upset the Rhythm).

   ( ) (   ) p   prototype
poetry / prose / interdisciplinary projects / anthologies

Creating new possibilities in the publishing of fiction and poetry
through a flexible, interdisciplinary approach and the production of
unique and beautiful books.

Prototype is an independent publisher working across genres and
disciplines, committed to discovering and sharing work that exists
outside the mainstream.
    Each publication is unique in its form and presentation, and the
aesthetic of each object is considered critical to its production.
    Prototype strives to increase audiences for experimental writing,
as the home for writers and artists whose work requires a creative
vision not offered by mainstream literary publishers.

In its current, evolving form, Prototype consists of 4 strands of
publications:
    (type 1 — poetry)
    (type 2 — prose)
    (type 3 — interdisciplinary projects)
    (type 4 — anthologies) including an annual anthology
    of new work, *PROTOTYPE*.

I'm Afraid That's All We've Got Time For by Jen Calleja
Published by Prototype in 2020

Design by Traven T. Croves
(Matthew Stuart & Andrew Walsh-Lister)
Cover illustration by Richard Phoenix
Typeset in Times New Roman
Printed in Lithuania by KOPA

ISBN 978-1-9160520-5-5

( )   (   )   p   prototype

(type 2 — prose)
www.prototypepublishing.co.uk
@prototypepubs

prototype publishing
71 oriel road
london e9 5sg
uk

(   )